Do Not Forsake Me, Oh My Darling

for Sonia

so nice to meet you again

All my best,

Maura

Notre Dame
Feb 8 2002

THE RICHARD SULLIVAN PRIZE IN SHORT FICTION

Editors
William O'Rourke and Valerie Sayers

Do Not
Forsake Me,
Oh My Darling

MAURA STANTON

University of Notre Dame Press
Notre Dame, Indiana

Published by University of Notre Dame Press
Notre Dame, Indiana 46556
http://www.undpress.nd.edu

Manufactured in the United States of America

Library of Congress Cataloging-in-Publication Data
Stanton, Maura.
Do not forsake me, oh my darling / Maura Stanton.
p. cm.—(The Richard Sullivan prize in short fiction)
ISBN 0-268-02555-X (cloth: alk. paper)
ISBN 0-268-02556-8 (pbk. : alk. paper)
I. Title.   II. Series.
PS3569.T3337 D6   2001
813'.54—dc21
2001003522

∞ *This book was printed on acid-free paper.*

For my mother
Wanda Haggard Stanton

Contents

Acknowledgments

The stories in this collection have appeared in the following publications.

"Do Not Forsake Me, Oh My Darling,"
   The Chariton Review
"Ping-Pong," *The Chicago Tribune*
"The Ugly Virgin," *Crab Orchard Review*
"The Cliffs of the Moon," *The Cream City Review*
"How to Converse in Italian," *North Dakota Quarterly*
"Marie Antoinette's Harp," *The Notre Dame Review*
"Squash Flowers," *Ploughshares*
"My Death," *Quarterly West*
"My Sister's Novel," *The Sycamore Review*
"The Cat and the Clown," *TriQuarterly*

"Do Not Forsake Me, Oh My Darling" was reprinted in *Lovers,* The Crossing Press, 1992.

Ping-Pong

The GI's, at this distance in time, all look alike, with the same smiling, intent, confident, innocent expressions—nice-looking young men, though a little thin because they are still recovering from wounds or fevers. Some are in uniform, some are in their pajamas and maroon bathrobes. You can tell by looking at them that they know how to tell jokes and would reach out and be glad to give you a cordial handshake if you were introduced, or offer you one of their precious cigarettes if they took a liking to you.

My father is sitting on a folding chair, leaning forward, looking intently at the woman in the center of the room. His lips are just about to smile as he listens, and I see the same expression of pleasure, an expression of hearing something funny and true, on the faces of the other men who all lean a little toward the woman.

Gertrude Stein is in profile, just raising her hand in a gesture to accompany something she's just said. Her suit jacket looks nubby, like linen, and she's wearing a scarf at her neck. She's taken off her winter coat, and it's spread out on the chair, the satin lining like a shiny pool all around her. At the corner of the photograph, Alice Toklas is just visible. Her face is out of focus, but you can see that she's holding two big purses on her lap, and one of them must be Gertrude Stein's. One black, lace-up shoe, pointing out, shines in the flash that washes out the front of the photograph.

The nurses are standing in the back of the room. My mother, taller and prettier than the others, her blond bangs in a swooping roll above her forehead, is looking at my father. This photograph was taken before he was promoted to lieutenant, and their engagement is still secret. My father, a medic, has recently been transferred from the 16th Station Hospital, where my mother is stationed, to the First General in Paris.

My father met Gertrude Stein at a New Year's Eve party for GI's. She'd come back to Paris after the liberation, and was going around cheering up the American troops. My father, always shrewd and quick-thinking, saw a chance to visit my mother. He talked to his Colonel (later the best man at my parents' wedding) and arranged to drive Gertrude Stein and her friend Alice Toklas out to the 16th Station Hospital in the Château Le Marais to visit the walking wounded.

What did she talk about that day? I can only guess as I sift through the other photographs of my parents' wartime years that my mother has mailed me in a shoe box, fairy-tale views of the Château Le Marais in the snow, with the lake in front and the moat and formal gardens in the back, or the photos of the village of Argentan, bombed into rubble, or the funny pictures of nurses in combat fatigues washing out underwear in helmets, and hanging it to dry on tent ropes. There's a photo of an operating theater divided into cubicles by hanging sheets, and a photo of wounded personnel—including several women—on stretchers waiting to be shipped home. My mother is moving to a small apartment in a senior citizens' tower, and has been sending me boxes of things she doesn't want to keep but can't bring herself to throw away. She's given me back my baby locket, with my teeth marks in the soft gold, years of homemade, yellowing Christmas cards I made out of construction paper in grade school, my old report cards, a recipe box I painted for her in Girl Scouts, a pair of crystal liqueur glasses I bought her with money from my first job at the department store, my ice skates from college, hardly used, the blades still wrapped in tissue, an antique silver candy dish that belonged to my grandmother, and my father's old twin-lens reflex camera.

When I was growing up, I did not make any distinction between the group photo that included Gertrude Stein and any of the other group photos of people my parents had met in the war. My father's colonel, with his small, stiff mustache, and my mother's best friend with her smooth pageboy, and the knots of young men and women in uniform all seemed equally strange and interesting to me. My mother or my father would point to this person or that person, and I'd learn that this officer was a psychiatrist, and that nurse came from Maine, and this orderly was a flirt, and that orderly had died of cancer in 1953, and that nurse had shared a tent with my mother, and that medic had been a Hollywood photographer before the war, and this old woman with short hair had arranged for my parents' civil marriage by the mayor of Paris, and the church wedding at the Madeleine. The fact that it was Gertrude Stein who had cut through the red tape to facilitate my parents' marriage escaped me for many years. They must have mentioned that she was a writer. But the wartime writer whose book they owned and admired was Ernie Pyle. A battered copy of *Here Is Your War* had a place of honor in our glass-fronted bookcase, shelved next to Dickens and Walter Scott.

Some curious line seemed to have been crossed forever when my parents returned to America, so that those handsome people who inhabited the black-and-white photos of the war years did not seem to resemble the bright, gaudy young marrieds of the postwar suburbs. I was always more interested in the stories or the details in the pictures than in the real names of the people, though I delighted in knowing that the swan on the lake was called Tallyrand. I asked about the color of the bathrobes worn by the recovering GI's, I dreamed of walking through the glassed-in arcade that connected the château to the servants' quarters where the nurses slept, I made my mother show me how to roll my bangs under like the nurses, and I made her sing me the words to the song, "And the Angels Sing," the tune she had urged wounded soldiers to hum when they were being put under ether in the field hospital after the Normandy invasion. I absorbed the atmosphere of the war.

But only my parents stood out as individuals.

When I was ten or eleven years old, I received a birthday present from my aunt Margie. When I opened the green Marshall Fields' box, I found a dress of polished cotton printed with roses, and around each rose in a circle were the words "a rose is a rose is a rose is a rose" that you could keep reading around and around forever. My father, standing behind the hassock where I sat, leaned down and fingered the dress, exclaiming in surprise:

"Why, I know who wrote that!"

"Really?" I said, lifting the dress and shaking away the tissue paper to admire the shirred front. "What's it mean, Dad?"

"No idea," he said. "I don't think she knew either. But while I was wasting time asking her about it, she beat me at Ping-Pong."

"She beat you? I thought nobody ever beat you."

"She did," my father laughed. "A rose is a rose is a rose is a rose."

I was delighted to think that somebody who wrote about a rose on my dress had actually beaten my father at something—no one had ever beaten my father at a game. He never let me win at Hearts or Crazy Eights or chess or Monopoly or badminton and especially Ping-Pong, which we used to play down in the basement, pocking the balls back and forth for a few minutes before he'd start hitting them hard past my head. So while I was growing up I carried around that little nugget of memory, that some woman who said a rose is a rose is a rose is a rose had played Ping-Pong with my father, and won. Later in college, when I discovered that the nugget was pure gold—that my father had been beaten in Ping-Pong by the famous writer, Gertrude Stein—it was too late. My father was dead.

"Château Le Marais, March 1945," I read in light pencil on the back of this next photo. My future parents, now that my father's been promoted, are posed in their winter army uniforms on the shore of the lake. Behind them is the swan they have named Tallyrand. My mother is holding up her left hand to show the camera the bright engagement ring that I'll see later on her finger, sparkling in the soapsuds as she does the dishes. The platinum wedding ring (it's impossible to get gold at this point in the war) has been mailed from Chicago, and is wrapped up in a chamois cloth in my father's footlocker in Paris. They hope to be married soon, but it's complicated. Army red tape is doubled by French red tape. But all will soon be well. Miss Stein is going to help.

I peer more closely at the photo. My father's mouth is shaped as if he's talking. Even as they stand there in the snow, my father may be telling my mother not to worry, that Gertrude Stein is talking to some top brass.

How many times, as my divorce was pending, did I go over to the end table in my living room, scarred with white rings from my soon-to-be ex-husband's gin and tonics, and pick up the framed picture of my parents in their army uniforms standing on the steps of the Madeleine on their wedding day? Gertrude Stein wasn't there—she was off visiting troops in occupied Germany—but according to my mother she'd spoken to this general who'd spoken to that general, she'd spoken to a priest who'd spoken to a bishop, and finally she'd spoken to an old friend in the F.F.I. who'd spoken to the mayor of Paris, and the mayor of Paris had agreed to perform the civil ceremony himself.

. . .

I usually mention this little incident quickly, with irony, but I want to try something different, because the more I think about it—and sorting through this box of photos is stirring me up—the irony came later. It wasn't there from the beginning.

So let me step back from myself, and see if I can dredge up my real feelings at the time.

A woman in her midthirties—someone with my coloring and height, who might be me but isn't because you can never see yourself objectively—arrives at Père-Lachaise Cemetery in Paris and passes through the iron gate. It's raining, but she buys the 10 franc map, locates the name Gertrude Stein, and heads up the Avenue Principale, taking long steps over puddles, tilting her umbrella against gusts of spray, holding her cellophane-wrapped bouquet of roses against her chest. What she is doing makes her feel funny and a little ashamed. She hasn't visited her father's grave since his burial in the Fort Snelling Veterans Cemetery years ago, when she handed the folded flag to her mother, took her arm, and steered her back to the car, leaving her father's silver coffin sitting on tresles under a canopy, surrounded by acres of identical small markers. But here she is, hurrying in the rain to visit the grave of the woman who beat him in Ping-Pong.

She's still getting used to being divorced. Her husband, a poet, had an affair last year. She came home early from her job at the art museum, heard the television going in the bedroom, and walked in just in time to see a pair of short, hairy, female legs sticking out of the quilt, and her husband coming out of the bathroom, naked, wiping himself with a towel. What made her really mad was that the girl was one of her husband's graduate students, and only two weeks ago she'd gone with her husband to hear the girl read a bunch of boring, surrealistic poems about the depressed inner lives of cartoon characters, and had even spoken to the girl afterwards, more out of pity than anything, telling her she liked her work.

She'd lost her temper. She'd screamed at the girl, who cowered before her, her sharp, bare shoulder blades almost touching her ears. At the time, the woman felt more upset by the fact that the girl was in her bed than she was by the fact that she'd screwed her husband, and later, after her husband had moved in with the girl, taking nothing but his books and clothes and the big-screen television he'd bought with his grant money, she tried to comfort herself with this notion, that she'd cared more about the violation of her personal space than she'd cared about the affair itself. She'd wadded up the sheets and thrown them in the trash.

But she was devastated. It was a month before she called home to tell her mother, who gasped, then sighed, then said several times, "Thank God your father isn't alive to hear this!" She urged her daughter to try to save her marriage through counseling. The woman listened to her mother's advice, but when she hung up, she just sat there looking at the phone, her hands blocks of ice, wondering how her husband could have preferred a short, dumpy, rat-faced, depressive kid who didn't shave her legs to a tall, blond, cheerful, intelligent woman who worked out every day. She started to shiver, and immediately her throat got sore. By that evening, she had a fever, and the beginning of the worst cold she'd ever had in her life.

It was her husband's moral vacillation that got to her the most. If she'd asserted herself, she could have got him to come home, and they could have resumed their life together, and she might have gotten used to his cool, drifty ways all over again, and learned to exercise more care, so that pushy, star-struck graduate students couldn't get their chewed fingernails into his soft back in the future. But that wasn't the kind of relationship she'd imagined when she was growing up. She'd wanted to fall in love with someone brave and confident and optimistic, a hero like the GI's in the WWII movies, not someone who wore untucked Hawaiian shirts and rubber thongs and sat reading literary magazines on the toilet for an hour every morning.

But back in 1973, when she'd met her husband in graduate school, men weren't like that. The Vietnam War was over, but, just as you get used to a stiff hinge on a door, so that even after you oil it with WD-40, you continue to pull it as hard as you used to, they still sneered at the establishment and baked whole wheat bread and wrote poetry and wore boots without socks and drove battered Volkswagens and kissed your toes when they made love and smiled dreamily when they passed you a joint. In snapshots from those days, she found it hard to distinguish her husband from his friends. They all looked alike, unsmiling behind their rimless glasses and big mustaches, their hair shaggy around their ears.

You didn't marry a man, she decided, you married a generation.

Here in Père-Lachaise she's seen enough pictures in books to know not to expect a fancy monument to Gertrude Stein, like the ones that crowd the avenues where a million people are buried in only 100,000 tombs. As she climbs to the back of the cemetery, leaving the Avenue Saint-Morys and crossing the Avenue Transversale, she passes miniature castles with turrets, tall obelisks, and huge angels, some with uplifted swords, some covering their faces with their wings in grief. Off the Avenue Circulaire she finds a grassy plot edged with limestone and a simple marker with Gertrude Stein's name, and Alice Toklas discreetly behind her. There are already roses on the grave, a dried, dead bouquet still wrapped in cellophane, and some long-stemmed yellow roses, the petals curled and browning, that someone has scattered.

One day, in an English class at the University of Minnesota, a year after her father had died suddenly of a heart attack, her only female professor, going over a list of suggested books for extra-credit reports, had quoted "a rose is a rose is a rose is a rose" in a bright, mocking voice when she came to *The Autobiography of Alice B. Toklas*. It's too bad, the professor went on, but newspapers and jealous critics have reduced the complexity of a great revolutionary writer to a little heading on her stationery.

The woman felt as if she'd been zapped by a volt of electricity. She remembered the words on her pink dress, a dress she had especially loved and worn to several birthday parties, and she remembered the photograph of a stout woman talking to GI's that she'd often studied on rainy days when she went through the albums and boxes of photos stored in the dining-room hutch, and she began to put two and two together. She called home that evening. Her mother confirmed that the writer, Gertrude Stein, had pulled some strings for her marriage, but she'd only met her that one time when she came out to the château. No, she didn't remember what she talked about. It was your father who was friends with her, she told her daughter, who asked about the Ping-Pong game. Her mother knew nothing about it. She could add nothing except to say that there were always Ping-Pong tables at Red Cross clubs, and that the match could have taken place anywhere.

And so the woman became obsessed with Gertrude Stein. She switched her major in college from English to Art History, because she liked the idea of becoming a collector, like Gertrude and her brother, Leo, and she paid $150 for an abstract painting at the graduate student art fair, and hung it in her dorm room. She went to graduate school at the University of Iowa, where she hung out with writers as well as painters, and her obsession with Gertrude Stein became a sort of joke with her friends, who gave her books by Gertrude Stein, and biographies of Gertrude Stein or her contemporaries like Picasso and Marie Laurencin and Apollinaire, for presents. Her future husband had located a copy of the hard-to-find *Brewsie and Willie* in a secondhand bookstore when he went to Chicago for a job interview. He didn't get the job, but two weeks later she herself was offered a job at a museum in the west, and they decided to get married. He talked of a ceremony in the woods with chanting and candles, and—he was grinning when he added this part—Alice B. Toklas' brownies. But she had the image of her parents on the steps of the Madeleine in the back of her head, and arranged to be married by a judge one Monday morning at the Johnson County Courthouse. One of their witnesses photographed them on the broad steps. Her husband wore white bell-bottoms and a tight tweed jacket borrowed from a friend. Her hair was rolled in front in the style of the 1940s. She wore a pink suit, and carried a bouquet of pink roses.

Just like the roses she's holding now. She stands there under her umbrella, wondering if she should pick up the browning roses on the grave, and the old bouquet, before leaving her own, or if she should simply scatter her fresh ones across the dead ones, the way new corpses are placed on top of old ones in the family sepulchers.

"A rose is a rose is a rose is a rose," she says softly to herself.

Then she hears a sound behind her.

As she jerks around, she's aware of two skinny young men in blue-jean jackets. Before she can open her mouth to ask what they want, her bag is ripped from her shoulder, and she's pushed hard to the ground. She falls directly onto Gertrude Stein's grave, her breath knocked out of her so that her scream emerges as an ineffectual squeak, and her open umbrella and the bouquet go flying out of her hands. She can hear footsteps pounding away.

Her chest hurts from hitting the ground so hard. There's wet grass in her mouth now. She sits up, but she's shaking so much she can't stand. Her bright red umbrella has bounced over to the next grave, and sits there like a huge tulip.

She knows there is no point in screaming. She hasn't passed anyone since leaving the Avenue Saint-Morys. The muggers must have been hiding behind a monument, waiting for someone to wander up to this deserted area. And she hasn't lost anything of value. Her passport and her traveler's checks and credit cards and most of her francs are safely in her money belt. All the muggers have got is a wallet with 20 francs, her hairbrush and lipstick, lots of tissues, and the map of the Père-Lachaise.

But she can't stop shaking. She stretches over and grabs her umbrella, and even though it's raining and she's getting soaked, she furls it shut and grasps it like a weapon. She gets to her feet, then looks down, noting that she's trodden on her own bouquet, crushing the roses.

Her teeth are chattering. She forces herself to recall the direction of the running footsteps for fear of encountering the muggers again, then starts walking fast the other way, heading down toward the entrance, cringing and hesitating whenever she sees someone among the monuments, then sprinting past. At the gate she pauses, then remembers that the dour man who sold her the map spoke no English, and knowing that she's too shaky to say anything coherent in her limited French, she walks on through. As soon as she steps out the gate, she's blasted by traffic noise. Her body feels stiff and bruised, and all she can think about is a hot bath. For the first time, she wonders how a heavy woman in her sixties could ever have beaten her tall, quick, young father in a game of Ping-Pong. Her father was probably joking, or she's mis-remembered what he said.

She walks back slowly to her hotel. Paris has lost its charm.

·   ·   ·

My parents swam at Juan les Pins on their honeymoon. The Carleton in Cannes had been turned over to the American Army for R & R for officers, and that's where they stayed. I remember some little miniature barrels of solid perfume on my mother's dressing table when I was very, very young, that she'd brought back from Grasse. I used to unscrew the top, and smear the brown, sweet-smelling wax on my face. She said I'd broken her beautiful cut-glass bottle of L'Heure Bleue that she'd been given for a wedding present by the head nurse, when I was three. I didn't remember doing it, but she'd tell me to sniff the cushion of her dressing-table stool if I wanted to know what it smelled like, and even in high school I'd sneak into her room and press my face against the faded blue brocade, close my eyes, and dream I was in Paris.

My parents returned home from Europe on separate troop ships. My mother packed her silk scarf from the Galeries Lafayette, her combat helmet, her photo album with Anne Hathaway's cottage on the cover that she'd bought when she was first stationed in Salisbury, England, and her French phrase book and her perfumes, and my father packed the German darning egg that had belonged to a German prisoner and a little book of Pascal's *Pensées* and a stack of black-and-white postcards with beveled edges, showing the Côte d'Azur before the war, and his snapshots of tanks and ruined villages that his unit had passed through. And they entered the world of SweetHeart Soap, Jewelite brushes, Calox Tooth Powder, Sunsweet Prune Juice, Simmons Electronic Blankets, Esterbrook fountain pens, Packard Clippers, Lifebouy Shaving Cream, Colgate Ribbon Dental Cream, Cat's Paw Rubber Heels, Unguentine, Blatz Beer, Scripto, and Lucky Strike, and because it was life, plain old everyday American life, they moved forward gladly into the new postwar world, and I came squalling into existence just like Casper the Friendly Ghost whooing out of the still frames of the Sunday funny papers into his first blaring animated cartoon.

I call my mother to tell her I've received the box of photographs.

"Good," she says. "You always liked to look at them more than I did. Is there any furniture you'd like me to keep for you? I'm going to get rid of a lot of stuff before you come up to help me move."

"What about the Ping-Pong table?" I ask her. "Remember how I used to play Ping-Pong with Dad?"

"The Ping-Pong table?" She sounds puzzled. "But you know I gave that to your cousin Matt twenty years ago!"

"Oh, I forgot," I say, feeling embarrassed. For of course I've been down in the basement at least once every time I've visited. How could I not remember that it's been replaced by the old dinette table, which my mother uses to store all the small appliances like ice-cream makers and breadmakers and waffle irons and coffee grinders and yogurt makers and cappuccino machines and food processors and knife sharpeners and lettuce spinners and woks and fondue pots that I've given her as presents over the years, that she has no room for up in the kitchen, and knows that she'll never use again after the first time?

"But speaking of Ping-Pong," my mother goes on, "years ago you asked me about Jack playing Ping-Pong with Gertrude Stein, and while I was cleaning out his old footlocker in the basement, I came across a notebook that he had during the war—it's mostly empty except for some addresses—but there's this one page near the beginning. Here, I'll read it to you."

The receiver clatters when she puts it down. Then she's back. I can hear rustling.

My mother clears her throat. She reads:

"'Played Ping-Pong with G. Stein. She asked a lot of questions about America. Then she said if I beat her, I had to pay a forfeit and call my first daughter Gertrude. So I let her win.'"

"Wow!" I say. "Is it dated?"

"No," my mother says. "And the next page is just some French verbs he was trying to learn. I'll send this to you. You can see for yourself."

When I hang up, I'm feeling more cheerful than I have in months. I stand looking out the picture window at our cactus garden, then I wander into the kitchen and decide I'll make Lenny some fresh salsa, something I haven't done for months, not since I fell into a fit of gloom when my mother said she was selling the house I grew up in, even though I haven't lived in it for thirty years. My parents' life always seemed like a romantic story in a book while I was growing up in that little house in Minnesota, while my own life here in Arizona, especially after my divorce and remarriage to an orthopedic surgeon with two teenage children, seemed so typical and ordinary it was inenarrable. That's a fancy word I came across recently. It means something that can't be narrated.

But now I see that my life may have a story after all, a story that began before I was even conceived. Nonexistent, uncreated, nameless, I was conjured up in France one winter day during a Ping-Pong game between my uniformed father and Gertrude Stein. Gertrude Stein briefly spoke of me, allowing me to exist, to flutter and struggle inside her playful wager, as she served the ball to my father. I'd like to imagine that she laughed when he made that goofy lunge with his paddle, and missed to let her win.

Squash Flowers

We were both sitting in old-fashioned green metal lawn chairs that rocked back gently on metal tube frames if you wanted them to, and I did. I rocked as I sipped the strong, lemony tea up through the straw, hoping Mrs. Eelpout would tell me a story. She was sniffling, still getting used to the news: Her friend and neighbor's cremated ashes had been found in a garbage can.

Mrs. Eelpout was wearing tortoiseshell glasses that swooped up at the corners, making her look like a lynx. The lenses seemed to be very, very, thick bifocals with wavy half-moons across the bottoms for reading. Her hand trembled as she placed her own glass on the wrought-iron table between us. I was afraid she might spill her tea on the tape recorder. It had taken me a while to convince Mrs. Eelpout to let me use it. Only when I'd insisted that nothing was left of poor Mrs. DiLuna, except for a few memories that might be lodged inside Mrs. Eelpout's own head, had she allowed me to switch it on.

"How could someone—her own son no less—do a thing like that?" Mrs. Eelpout smoothed the apron that she'd put on, for ceremonial purposes, when she went inside the trailer to pour the tea. The apron was clean and pressed, but so worn that the pattern of tiny pink flowers had almost washed away. She'd been shocked at first, then angry, and then weepy when I told her how the new people renting my trailer had found a brass-cornered wooden box in the garbage can out back, containing the cremated remains of her friend.

"Did she ever talk about her last wishes?" I asked. The expression, which I had never used before, felt puckery in my mouth like a bite of grapefruit.

"Sure she did," Mrs. Eelpout said. "She talked about her last wishes and I talked about mine. She wanted to be buried back east beside her second husband, just like I want to be buried up the hill there in the Abode of Bliss Cemetery, right between my mama and Mr. Eelpout. Why, she had her plot waiting for her, the headstone carved and everything, she told me. Now why couldn't they do that for the poor old thing?"

"Money, probably," I said. "They skipped town after the cremation, leaving lots of debts. They never paid the funeral home. They didn't even call an ambulance—they were driving her to the hospital in the next county after she'd had a stroke when she died of congestive heart failure in the backseat, at least that's what the coroner's report says." I leaned forward, checking to make sure the volume on the machine was turned high enough. "And when they got the cremated ashes from the funeral home, they just dumped the box in the garbage can and cleared out, knowing they couldn't pay the bills."

"We were summer friends," Mrs. Eelpout said, shaking her head. "I never stepped foot inside that trailer. Her son's wife, that Sherrie, would help her outside, and she'd settle down right in that very chair you're sitting in. Sherrie'd put an afghan over Mrs. DiLuna's lap, and I'd make some tea, just like now. We'd sit here talking for hours whenever it was fine, listening to the birds, watching things poking up in my little garden. Those were the flowers she loved best." Mrs. Eelpout pointed at some yellow flowers that looked like trumpets, growing up along the edge of the trailer.

"What are they?" I asked.

"Squash flowers—zucchini. But I never get any zucchini. You need the right bee to come along, they say. I wouldn't have bothered with them this year, but I knew Mrs. DiLuna doted on them, and I thought I'd be seeing her again once the weather turned fine. I thought she'd be looking forward to coming outside after being cooped up in that trailer all winter."

"So you didn't visit her in the winter?"

"Once I put on my boots and tramped over—it was before Christmas, and I had a little poinsettia for her—but that woman, that Sherrie, told me she wasn't feeling well. She just took the plant and didn't even invite me in for a moment. I tried calling once, on her birthday in February, but they told me she was too weak to talk on the phone. I knew she was frail. Sometimes when they brought her outside near the end of last summer she was all out of breath. It'd be an hour before she'd be able to say anything."

"Do you think she belonged in a nursing home?"

Mrs. Eelpout sniffed loudly. "I don't wish a nursing home on any poor soul. At least they brought her outside in the fine weather. But not this year. I called to that woman once when she was getting into her car, how's his mama, I called, and she waved, and said, she's pretty poorly, the air might be too much for her this summer. I felt bad. I'd already put in my squash flowers. Then two weeks ago I saw all that trash out front, and the venetian blinds off the windows. I thought they'd just moved in the night, and taken poor Mrs. DiLuna along with them." She lifted the corner of her apron, and dabbed at her eyes. "I had a good cry. Moved away, and we never got to say good-bye. And now this."

The evening sky was a thick eggwhite color. The yellow squash flowers were beginning to shrink and close like balloons leaking air. I could almost see them trembling before my eyes. A dove called from the single pine tree that had not been cut down when the trailer court was opened. Back when Denny and I had lived here, before we moved to the new house and began to rent the trailer, we had called it our lonesome pine because we had a view of it from our tiny bedroom window when we made love.

"She was a sweet thing, Minnie was," Mrs. Eelpout said, clearing her throat and looking down at the tape recorder. "We called each other by our first names when we were alone together, you see. She always called me Willa. Willa, she'd say, you do grow the most beautiful zinnias and bachelor buttons. When they first moved in here, it was two summers ago, I couldn't get over the three of them when they got out of the car, that son of hers, Nick, with the ugly wolf tattooed on one shoulder, and that Sherrie, his wife, with her big puffed-up hair, like a high-school girl's with a bow on the top and she almost fifty, and then poor sweet Minnie, her snow-white hair curled like a little lamb's back, trotting behind them with her walker, which they hauled out of the trunk for her. She always had trouble with those steps to the trailer over there—they're not a natural size, I don't think."

I looked over at the trailer. I remembered those steps. I'd even fallen down them once when I'd had too much to drink. Luckily there'd been a deep snowfall, so I'd only landed on my face in a drift. Now I realized we should have called in a carpenter. I hated being a landlady. The only time I'd ever seen Mrs. DiLuna was the time I'd gone over to unstop the sink. Sherrie had leaned against the counter, eating Pringles one by one out of a red can as I worked the plunger, pulling up goop. Afterwards, I'd noticed a mound of blankets on the sofa. It seemed to be moving.

"Nick's mom," Sherrie had said, gesturing with a chip. And I'd seen a tiny little face peeping out at me. I didn't know if she could see me or not, but I smiled. A tiny, crooked hand was clutching the satin edge of one of the blankets.

Denny said he'd seen her a couple of times, when he was over doing repairs. He'd seen her bundled up in a lawn chair one afternoon. We didn't even know her name until the ashes turned up, and the sheriff got on the case. I felt especially bad because I wrote about interesting people for the Life Style page of our local paper. She hadn't seemed interesting, so I'd ignored her.

But the idea that somebody could end up as ashes in some old battered garbage can really bothered me. My God, she had a life, I told Denny, ninety years of life and now there's nothing? Is that possible?

He looked at me, nodding wisely, and when I made that little high-pitched shriek he hates so much, that I can't help making when something really gets to me, he said, why don't you go ask around the trailer court, if that'll make you feel any better?

All right, I will, I said. And here I was.

Mrs. Eelpout spread her hands out over her knees, and took a deep breath. Her nails were bitten down to the bright pink quick, and it startled me that someone would still be biting her nails in her eighties. I was a nail biter myself, and I kept thinking I'd outgrow the habit. Now I suddenly realized that I never would.

"My memory's not what it was," Mrs. Eelpout said. "We talked about a lot of things, and sometimes we didn't talk at all. But those squash flowers—" she lifted one big hand and waved it over in the direction of the shriveled yellow trumpets, "they'll always remind me of her."

.   .   .

Minnie—her real name in Italian was Dominica, Mrs. Eelpout said—had been taken out of the village school in Sicily when she was nine, and trained to be the cook and housekeeper for the whole family, her father and mother, her seven brothers and sisters, and her grandparents. When they all emigrated to America, she'd been excited, thinking they were going to a place where she'd get to live a real life like the kind she saw flickering by in the wonderful movies that were shown in the town hall on Sundays after the Angelus. She wanted her lips to be shaped like a bow, and her thick, waist-length hair cut so that it swung against her chin. But nothing changed for her in the new country. Her family lived far out in the sticks, beyond the Baltimore streetcar line; her father beat her and cuffed her just like he had in Sicily, only now there wasn't a village well she could dart down to every day and use as an excuse for exchanging complaints and gossip with other girls and women, and the long cold winter, with its constant rain squalls off the Atlantic, and the occasional heavy snow-falls, seemed endless.

Gardening was one of her jobs on the farm—in the spring she had to do the hoeing and plant the vegetables and do all the weeding, but she welcomed the work, because it took her away from her father's malevolent reach for most of the day. Suppers were a nightmare. She hadn't cooked the spa-ghetti al dente, the way he liked it, he said, or else he com-plained about too much salt in the soup. She usually got a box on the ear, or a slap across the mouth. Later, when she was grown and married, she hated cooking, and all her meals came from Betty Crocker or Kraft.

Once, back in Sicily, she'd planted some lavender and wild carnations in a little plot just for herself. One day her father, tramping about to see if she was keeping after the weeds, had discovered her flowers. His face turned almost maroon. How dare she waste her time on what wasn't edible? He brought shovels full of ash from the outdoor oven, and dumped them over the bright flowers until they all disap-peared into a sooty mound while she stood there watching helplessly, and then he took off his belt and whacked her over the shoulders until she fell face down in the carrots.

After that, she used to plant row after row of zucchini, because of the yellow flowers. She'd go out into the garden after supper, pretending she was plucking lettuce, and she'd admire their beauty, and when she came back to the house, she kept her eyes lowered, so that her father could not see that anything had given her pleasure.

In Maryland, the rich soil felt light and full of air. It did not have the cloying, putrid odor of the Sicilian dirt, turned over every year until it seemed sour, full of rotted tomatoes and moldy, hairy tubers. She dropped her zucchini seeds, a new American variety, into the raked rows, afraid they wouldn't come up for her, but to her joy they sprouted and grew into plants larger than she'd ever seen before. The flowers bloomed, showy as orchids, and she had never seen such firm, perfectly striped zucchini.

She was sixteen. She was assigned to serve dinner to the large table of shouting, drunken men who had gathered to help pick the tomatoes that August. The trestle table was set out under the concord grape arbor, and she had to go back and forth to the house with platters of spaghetti and big tureens of puttanesca sauce. There were jugs of red wine on the table. Some of the older men had faces like twisted pumpkins; the younger men had shiny hair the color of eggplants, and they pinched her bottom when she passed by them, if her father wasn't looking. But he was drunk, roaring out jokes and singing snatches from operas. Years afterwards, she'd switch off the radio if she caught even one line of an aria, hating opera as much as she hated the Italian language after she'd learned to speak English.

She'd just returned with another basket of bread when her father's arm lashed out and caught her as if she'd been prey for a crab.

"Here's your wife, Mario," he shouted, pushing her into the arms of a middle-aged man with a thick neck. He was their richest neighbor. His wife had died the year before. She'd seen him looking at her in church.

Now he kissed her so hard that her lips were bruised the next day, shouting as she struggled to get away, "My little anchovy, my little radicchio, I could eat you up!"

"When's the wedding?" somebody shouted.

"Next month she'll be cooking Mario's dinner," her father cackled. "And I'll be admiring my new apple trees."

She knew then that she was being traded for the orchard he coveted, which bordered their own property.

That night she couldn't sleep. She lay very still on her back, her head like a wooden block on the pillow, listening to her sister breathing in the other cot. She decided to kill her father as soon as the house was quiet.

The rifles were kept upright in a rack at the foot of the stairs. She was used to seeing things killed. Her father was always bringing down crows, or lugging bloody rabbits back from the fields. She had seen him put the muzzle of his rifle against the head of an old lame horse that couldn't work anymore, and she had not turned her eyes away at the spewing blood and matter when the bullet exploded. She had helped her brothers push the horse into the pit they had dug down near the creek. Her father had taught her to chop the heads off chickens back in Sicily, guiding her small, horrified hands with his huge, leathery paws.

She knew he had passed out in his favorite chair in the front room. She could hear his rolling snores. Her older brothers were drunk, too, sprawled face down on the cots in their own room, and her mother was in the bedroom across the hall, the quilt wrapped around her head.

She waited. She felt disembodied, neutral. She had no emotions. There was merely an action to perform, and then she would be free. She knew they would put her in jail, maybe hang her after a trial, but it was better not to try to imagine anything beyond the act she had to perform.

Her sister was breathing gently, her face buried in her hair. She got out of bed so as not to disturb her, and quickly dressed in the dark. She looped her high-topped shoes around her neck by their laces, and stuffed a pair of cotton stockings into her pocket. Was she going to run away afterwards? Her life seemed like a fantasy to her. She did not know who was in charge, her will or her body.

At the bottom of the stairs, she put her hand on the stock of a rifle. But as she touched the smooth wood, a vibration went through her, as if the gun had just fired, and she had to bite her lip to keep from crying out.

She couldn't kill him. She must have only dreamed that she was going to kill him. She felt clammy and frightened.

A snort that sounded like it came from a mule loose in the house made her jump back. It was her father. She held her breath until the regular snores resumed.

But the sound brought her back to herself. She couldn't kill him, but she had to do something. She had to get away from this place tonight.

The only place she could think of to go, the only place that in any way belonged to her, besides the bedroom that she shared with her sister, was her garden.

The moonlight shining through the thin clouds seemed especially bright when she stepped outside the kitchen door, careful to make no noise. She could hear the chickens clucking and rustling in the pen. The dog had been tied up in the barn, and his sporadic barks meant nothing. She might be a passing fox or an owl. She found a gunnysack in the shed, then slipped into the garden.

Dew was already coming up from the ground, thick as tears in the grass. Her bare feet were wet. She felt a snail under her toe, and drew her foot back before she crushed it. She went down the rows of her zucchini plants, and picked every one, no matter the size. She found one last yellow flower still blooming. She hesitated, then put it behind her ear. She heaved the sack over her shoulders.

At the crossroads, she waited for the first wagon to pass on its way to Baltimore with fresh produce. She waved to the man, who pulled up his chuffing team, and leaned down, sweeping off his battered felt hat as if to hear her better. She asked him if he wanted to buy some zucchini?

He looked at her curiously, pulling at his mustache. He named a price that was so low that she waved him on, and he shrugged, swirling his whip over his bony horses.

She stopped other wagons. The men were cheeky, and she held herself rigidly, not looking after them as they laughed and pulled away.

An hour later, a young man with distinct, fresh eyebrows, as mobile as caterpillars, agreed to her price. He also agreed to give her a ride into Baltimore, and helped her climb up onto the seat beside him. He tossed the sack of zucchini into the back of the wagon, on top of his bushel baskets of tomatoes, and as they clopped slowly toward the city, glowing with new electric lights in the distance, he told her about his sisters, Concetta and Angelica, and how they both worked in the candy factory, where he was sure they could find her a job, too, stirring the vats of chocolate or nougat, or hand-dipping the cherries or nuts, or even placing the cooled candies into the little crinkled papers inside fresh white boxes.

And at night, they would let her bring home the little damaged chocolates to eat for herself.

She could go walking to the movies arm in arm with Concetta and Angelica.

On warm nights, she could sit out on the white marble steps and listen to someone down the street play the accordion. Perhaps she would even let him sit beside her, he said softly, and she looked up. Wasn't that star the morning star?

She sat there, looking into the misty distance as she listened to the clop-clop of the horses' hooves carrying her away from a nightmare in which she had almost murdered her father, and into a dream of the future—movies and chocolates and row houses with marble steps all mixed together in her sleepy head. A whole long wonderful life stretched ahead of her.

Many years later, married to the man who had helped her escape from home, she'd still sometimes wake with a start in her mortgaged row house beside Memorial Stadium, thinking that she'd just blown her father's head off with a rifle. She'd sit up in bed, clammy in her nightgown, and hug her knees beside her snoring husband, forcing herself to remember how she'd reluctantly gone back to the farm to visit her father on his deathbed. He'd been in a coma, his withered face slack and his breathing raspy. He had not recognized her, but she had knelt at the foot of his four-poster bed along with her frail mother and her spinster sister and her pregnant sisters-in-law, saying the rosary, and she'd wept at his funeral like all the other women. Then, to push away the last cobwebs of the nightmare before she dared to curl back into sleep, she'd remind herself of the moment when she'd lifted her son— the spitting image of his grandfather according to all the relatives—up to view the coffined face. The boy had struggled in her arms for a moment, not wanting to look, and then at last he'd peeped, frowned, and stuck out his tongue.

Marie Antoinette's Harp

Saturday evening Jen walked to the opera by herself. She and her fiancé had season tickets for the University Opera Series, but Craig was out of town that weekend. At first she hadn't planned on going, but her happiness made her restless. She couldn't stay home on such a lovely spring night. So what if her pupils were still dilated from the drops they'd put in at the Optometry School Eye Clinic that afternoon? One of the things she liked about living in a college town was that she could walk everywhere she wanted to go. She didn't have to risk driving with blurry vision.

It had been a perfect April day. She'd ordered her wedding cake in the morning, turning the pages of the caterer's glossy book to choose a dream of a cake, five tiered layers with gorgeous sugar roses and tiny stems and leaves of delicate spearmint. The butter-frosting braid around the edges of each layer would be studded with candied violets, and on the top, instead of a pair of stiff-looking bride and groom dolls, she'd selected a spray of fresh iris. After she'd ordered the cake, she'd had lunch with her old friend from high school, Sarah, still unmarried, who'd asked her for details about her May wedding with just the right tone of eagerness and envy.

The eye exam—she was getting new contacts—had lasted three hours because the optometry students had to get their work checked by the faculty doctors, but she hadn't minded. She'd asked a lot of questions about the various programs at the Optometry School. She worked as a recruiter for the university, and the more she knew, the more convincing she could be when she talked to prospective students and their parents.

The weather was so lovely that when she started to get ready for the opera she reached right past all the wool and corduroy in her closet and pulled out a light silk dress dotted with seashells. She put on white stockings and her new shoes. She couldn't see herself very well because of the eyedrops, but she twirled around a couple of times in front of her two cats who were sprawled on the bed after their dinners.

She left her apartment building a little early so she could take her time and walk to campus through the nice neighborhoods where the grass was turning a tender green. As she turned into Hawthorne, she spotted a "For Sale" sign, and stopped to look up at a big brick house with a tile roof and a balcony. She knew it was much too expensive for them right now—Craig was still in graduate school and designed software on the side—but it was exactly the kind of house she wanted to live in some day. She and Craig had been going around with a real estate agent for six months now, and just for fun they sometimes looked at a house that was far more than they could afford.

A bus from the retirement community was letting off senior citizens in front of the Musical Arts Center. The grey-haired women were still in their winter coats, but the younger women coming across from the parking lot, or down one of the campus walks, were dressed in flowery skirts or filmy dresses, and their bare arms and shoulders gleamed as they stepped into the lobby lights.

At the first intermission Jen floated among the chattering groups in the lobby, occasionally smiling or waving at an acquaintance who smiled or waved at her, but not stopping to talk to anyone. She noticed a glass display cube that she'd never seen before, and strolled over to look at it. Inside the cube was a small antique harp. There was a white card explaining the harp down in the corner, but even though she stooped and squinted, she couldn't read it. The eye doctor had told her that she'd be unable to read for several hours.

When she looked up, she noticed a small woman with dark frizzy hair staring at her through the harp strings on the other side of the glass cube. The woman caught her eye, and smiled. Then she came around the side of the cube.

"It's amazing, isn't it? Marie Antoinette's harp."

"Yes," Jen said. She couldn't place the woman, who seemed about ten years older than her. She must have met her on some committee.

"I took your advice, Jennifer," the woman said. "I got the divorce."

Jen stared at her. "What?"

The woman laughed. "Have you forgotten? That's all right. It was three years ago."

"I'm sorry," Jen said, shaking her head. "I really don't remember."

"We were both taking the van to the airport. I told you what happened and you told me I should divorce him. Well, I did."

Jen struggled to remember. She traveled a lot as a recruiter, and she often took the van to the airport that was fifty miles away. She enjoyed talking to people, all kinds of people, and she was a good listener. And yes, sometimes in the course of talking people asked for advice about this or that. But she did not remember advising anyone to get a divorce.

"I'm glad things worked out," she said.

"Would you like to go for cappuccino after the opera? That place across the street is nice. You're not with anyone, are you?"

"No," Jen said, wishing for the first time since she'd arrived at the opera that Craig was sitting in the empty seat beside her.

"Great!" The woman nodded. "I'll meet you here after the last act. You don't seem to remember my name. I'm Alena." She looked again at the harp. "This is beautiful, isn't it? Someone must have donated it recently. Imagine Marie stretching out her pretty white arms to pluck those strings. She had no idea what was going to happen to her in a few years!"

Alena laughed.

Jen smiled at her, a sinking sensation in her chest. She just wanted to go home after the opera. Her cats were waiting for her.

The lights flickered.

"We'd better get back to our seats," Jen said.

"We'll meet right here," the woman said, touching Jen's arm lightly with her hand.

During the second act, Jen kept crossing and recrossing her legs. Then it came to her. It was that time three years ago when she flew to Portland. There'd been a woman who started sobbing on the seat beside her in the back of the airport van. She'd just discovered her husband and another woman making love. Her husband thought she'd already left for the airport, that was it, but she'd forgotten something, Jen couldn't remember what, and had stopped at home to pick it up.

When the curtain went down, Jen stayed in her seat instead of walking out to the lobby for the intermission. She tried to read the synopsis of the third act, but all she could make out in the program was THE TALES OF HOFFMANN in bold type on the cover and INTERMISSION, ACT III on the inside. When the curtain rose she watched a gondola dock at a palace full of languorous men and women in shimmering clothes, but she had no idea what was going on. She closed her eyes and let her mind be swept along by the music. She imagined dancing with Craig cheek to cheek on a dark stage in a bright beam of light. The doctor had shone a bright beam of light into her eyes as she sat in his dark cubicle. He had lightly touched her face, lifting her eyelid. She wondered what Craig was doing now. The software convention was in San Francisco. Was he looking out at the lights of the city from his hotel room? Had he showered? Was he getting into bed?

At last the final curtain fell. She decided to tell Alena that she was too tired to go for coffee.

Alena was standing next to the harp. She looked small and forlorn in her long flowered skirt, and there were goosebumps on her thin bare arms. When she caught sight of Jen, she stepped forward eagerly, and Jen smiled back. So OK, Jen thought, one cappuccino and that's that.

. . .

The Dream Cafe smelled of coffee beans and cinnamon when they stepped through the door. Jen was surprised when Alena walked past some empty tables near the espresso machine, and led her down a corridor into the smoky bar section where all the tables seemed to be full. Then a group of laughing women got up from a booth, and Alena darted past a server with a long braid down her back who was holding a tray of beer mugs. She slid into the booth, and Jen slid in across from her. The bench was warm from the women who had just left.

"They make their own beer now," Alena said. "It's good stuff."

Jen looked around doubtfully. People were smoking and laughing and stamping their feet to the lively Celtic music being played on the small stage on the other side of the bar.

When the set was over, she could hear distorted French from the sound track of the movie showing in the back room.

"Will they serve cappuccino back here?" she asked.

"Sure. But I'm going to buy you an Irish coffee," Alena said. "That sounds better, doesn't it?"

"Fine," Jen said. "But I can't stay long."

Alena nodded. "You're always in a hurry. I've passed you a few times on campus. You walk so fast. You never noticed me."

"I guess not," Jen said.

"I've been wanting to talk to you." Alena leaned forward, her elbows on the table. "I wanted to tell you about my new life."

Jen drew a deep breath. "Listen, I don't know anything about your old life. I barely remember our conversation."

"I know," Alena said. "That's what's so amazing and mysterious. My whole life changed because of you, and you know nothing about it."

The server stopped by their booth. Jen looked at Alena's flushed face and shining eyes as she ordered Irish coffee. She knew she ought to leave right then and there, but her legs felt heavy, and she found herself leaning back in the booth instead. It was the way she had felt at the eye clinic when they told her to put her chin on the chin rest, and press her forehead against the bar. She had something in the back of her eyes, some old scars from a disease caused by fungus, and the eye doctor called in several of the optometry students to look at the phenomena. Then he sent her into another room and had a student photograph her eyes.

"Did you like the opera?" Alena leaned forward, her elbows on the table. A large diamond ring glittered on her finger, and Jen looked at it, trying to figure out if that was Alena's right hand or left hand. She imagined herself sitting on the other side of the table . . . the left hand, then. Alena had not moved her wedding ring to the right hand after the divorce.

"Yes," Jen said. "But that last act was confusing. What was that mirror for?"

Alena smiled. "It was a magic mirror. The courtesan was trying to steal Hoffmann's reflection. That happened to me once." She seemed to notice Jen staring at her ring, and began to twist it around and around her finger. "When I was packing to move out of the house, I went into the bathroom to get my toothbrush. I happened to look into the mirror over the sink, but there was nothing there, just the room behind me. Maybe you'll say it was just the light coming in the stained-glass window, or maybe I was just crying so hard the tears blurred my vision, but that's not the way it seemed at the time. I thought she'd stolen my reflection. I fainted, and hit my head on the Jacuzzi." She pushed the hair away from her forehead to show Jen a pink mark. "Look, you can still see the scar."

"You found them in the Jacuzzi, didn't you?" Jen said dreamily.

The muscles in Alena's neck went rigid. She strained forward. "You do remember. I thought so."

"It just came to me," Jen said, "when you mentioned the Jacuzzi. I really had forgotten."

"It was in the Jacuzzi all right. I was going to leave for the airport from my office, so he didn't expect me at home. But I'd forgotten the notes for the talk I was giving. They were in my desk in my study, so I cut a meeting. I got the notes, then I thought I heard voices. He wasn't supposed to be home. I threw open the bathroom door and there they were, naked in the water with all the candles burning. She saw me first, and yelled something in French."

"She's French?" Jen asked.

Alena nodded. "He took a night class and she was the instructor. I was supposed to take the class, too, but they put me on the tenure committee that semester, and it would have been too much work." She seemed about to say more when the server appeared with the Irish coffee, and set the glasses down on little paper rounds.

Jen warmed her hands around her hot glass, and sipped at the whipped cream. "This is going to sound strange," she said, "but you said there was a stained-glass window in your Jacuzzi room?"

"Yes. Did I tell you that before?"

"I don't think so," Jen said. "But a few months ago I saw a Jacuzzi room with a stained-glass window. My fiancé and I are planning to buy a house, and we've been looking at places."

"That was our house. He bought me out during the divorce settlement, and now he's selling it," Alena said. "What did you think of it?"

Jen hesitated. The house had struck her as gloomy, with a carpeted basement full of damp books, and an upstairs used for storage. The living room had been almost empty of furniture, while the master suite had been crammed with stuff—a TV, a computer station, even a microwave—as if the owners spent all their time in bed. The Jacuzzi tub had been dark blue, speckled with pubic hairs.

"It was too expensive for us," she said in a moment.

"It's already sold. I saw the sign today. He and she are going to Paris for a year and when they come back they're going to buy a new place." Alena took a deep gulp of her Irish coffee. When she set down the glass, she looked directly at Jen. "She's stolen my life."

"How could she steal your life?" Jen stared back at her. "You're sitting right here. This is your life."

Alena shook her head. "He and I used to dream of going to live in France together—we'd sell the house and move. We had lots of dreams—we were going to take flying lessons, we were going to hike in the Alps, we were going to buy a vineyard, we were going to do this, we were going to do that. And we did nothing, and that was OK, we were happy, I thought. And then I opened the door to the Jacuzzi room."

Alena finished the rest of her Irish coffee. "You know, I have this recurring dream where I'm standing outside that door, and I haven't opened it yet, and I turn away and I don't open it."

"But it was your own house," Jen said. "You had to open the door."

"That's what you told me before. You said that in my place you'd dump him like a rotten vegetable."

"Look," Jen said, sitting forward on the bench. "I was just being sympathetic. I was just saying what I thought you wanted me to say. That's what you get when you tell your troubles to strangers." She looked at her watch. "Listen, it's late. I've really got to go."

"Wait. There they are." Alena's face lit up. "Bob! Françoise! Over here."

A man and a woman, part of the crowd flowing out of the back room after the movie, stopped at the booth.

"Please join us," Alena said, sliding off her bench and gesturing for the couple to sit down. "This is my friend, Jennifer. We've been to the opera."

The man, who had receding salt-and-pepper hair, looked uneasily at the woman. She smiled, touched the man's hand reassuringly, and slid into the booth. He sat next to her.

Jen realized that she was going to have to slide further down her own bench in order to let Alena sit next to her. She felt trapped.

"I really have to go," she said, trying to get up.

"Oh, have a drink with us first," Alena said brightly, sitting down on the edge of the booth and pushing her shoulder against Jen's shoulder. Jen realized that she'd have to slide down or get into an embarrassing struggle with Alena.

She slid down and leaned against the far wall of the booth while Alena ordered another round of Irish coffees.

"This is my ex-husband, Bob," Alena said, when the server left. "And his wife, Françoise."

"Nice to meet you," Jen mumbled. This woman was about ten years younger than Alena. She had high cheekbones, and wore her blond hair shoulder length.

"I saw your car in the lot," Alena said. "I thought you'd be at the film. How's your French coming, Bob?"

"*Pas mal*," Bob said, his face reddening.

"I saw the 'Sold' sign."

"Yes, at last," Françoise said.

"Maybe I'll move to France, too," Alena said.

Françoise and Bob looked at each other. They didn't say anything.

"I'd like to do some research on Marie Antoinette," Alena continued. "Do you know they have her harp across the street?"

"Marie Antoinette's harp? How interesting," Françoise said.

"Hmm, Marie Antoinette's harp," Bob repeated. "I heard they're putting on *The Ghosts of Versailles* next season. They must be trying to drum up business."

Alena leaned forward. "I wonder if they let her have the harp in the dungeon? That's what I'd like to find out. Did she play it down there in the dark before they cut her head off? Or did they refuse to let her bring it along when they arrested her? Did she just sit there in the dark dreaming about her past life when she was happy and lived in the palace and played the harp and walked in the garden? She was only thirty-eight when they guillotined her—my age exactly."

Bob leaned forward, clearing his throat. "Look, Alena, if you have something to say, come right out and say it."

Alena leaned across the table. "I just wanted to tell you, Bob, that I had the funniest sensation when I was looking at Marie Antoinette's harp. I felt as if I'd just learned that Marie Antoinette was dead, and that three years ago, back when we were still married, she'd been alive. Which is nonsense, of course. She was just as dead three years ago as she is now."

"I'd better go," Jen said. "It looks like you people have stuff to talk over."

"We don't have any stuff to talk over—nothing that you can't hear, Jennifer," Alena said, patting Jen's shoulder. "You're the one who advised me get a divorce. If it wasn't for you, he and I would still be married."

Jen flushed. Her throat tightened in anger. "That's nonsense!"

"Jennifer's good with people," Alena said, letting her hand fall away from Jen's shoulder. "She loves to give advice."

The server appeared with a tray of foamy glasses. She set them down carefully while Jen fumbled for money in her purse. By the time she found her wallet in the bottom, Alena had handed over her credit card.

"These are on me," she said.

Now Alena had her elbows on the table, effectively blocking Jen's exit from the booth. Jen grabbed her Irish coffee and took a deep gulp, burning her throat.

Françoise caught Jen's eye. She rolled her eyes to indicate that she, too, thought Alena was crazy. Bob was staring down at the table.

"You *are* good with people, aren't you, Jennifer?" Alena said, speaking close to Jen's ear and dropping her voice almost to a whisper, so that Françoise had to lean forward a little to catch what she was saying, and Bob lifted his head and opened his mouth as if to interrupt his ex-wife, but didn't.

"You're outgoing and social and friendly and nice and full of empathy and concern and goodwill and everybody likes you and thinks you're great and wonderful," Alena continued. "I've asked people in your office about you, you know. 'Oh, Jen, she's a super person.' 'Oh, Jen, she's terrific.' And you think you are, too, you think you're nice and kind and warmhearted, don't you? Well, I'll tell you what you are. Underneath you don't give a fucking damn about anyone but yourself. You don't give a fuck that you've ruined my life."

"I don't have to listen to this," Jen said. She could feel her face getting red. "Let me out of here."

Alena did not move. Jen pushed against her, but she went on talking. "You don't believe you had anything to do with it, do you, even though you were the one who told me I should divorce him? That's what you'd do if you were me, you said. Look at you. You're pissed off because I'm telling you the truth. Do you know what Marge said about you? Marge, the secretary who works in your office? You're all nice and smiley and friendly-like and ready with your advice, but if anybody has any real problems like their husband gets cancer and they aren't promoted when they should be, you get this glazed look on your face and mumble a few platitudes and that's that. You don't give a damn about anyone but yourself."

Jen felt light-headed. All around her people were stamping their feet and whistling and clapping their hands to a lively Celtic jig that the button accordionist had just begun to play. Alena kept on with her tirade, though most of her hissing words were lost in the cheerful din. Bob kept muttering, "For God's sake, Alena, for God's sake." He was still looking at the table, but Françoise had her hands over her mouth, and her eyes closed, as if she were going to throw up.

"If you don't get up and let me out of here," Jen said, "I'm going to crawl out under the table."

"Wait," Alena said. "Look at these first." She reached into her purse on the floor and quickly brought out an envelope. She dumped a stack of color snapshots across the table and fanned them out. Jen glanced down at them. The photographs were all of Alena and Bob. In some of them they had their arms around each other and were standing in front of a big Christmas tree. In others they were standing on a beach or next to a saguaro cactus or a redwood trunk or looking out at a view from a mountaintop. In some photos Bob's hair was thick and black, and Alena's hair was long and shining and her face was smooth and round. In others they were older. Bob's hairline had receded. Alena had lines around her eyes.

"This is the life you advised me to give up, Jennifer," Alena said, pointing to one of the Christmas trees.

Jen followed Alena's finger. She looked at the presents piled under the tree at the feet of the smiling couple.

"I'm not feeling well," Françoise said, grabbing Bob's arm.

"We're going, Alena," Bob said. He looked at Jen. "I'm sorry about this. She's depressed. We've advised her to see a counselor. It has nothing to do with you."

"Let me out," Jen said. "Please."

Alena shrugged. Then in one quick movement of her hand she swept all the snapshots onto the floor. She almost leapt out of the booth. She stood beside the table, her head down. Jen grabbed her purse, slid out, and darted away. She did not look back.

But she'd headed the wrong direction, toward the rear of the Dream Cafe. She did not want to pass that table again, so she ducked into the women's restroom. Two girls with buzz cuts and tattoos on their bare shoulders stood at the sinks, one of them with her head tilted back, holding something against her nose, and the other leaning over her. Jen quickly opened a stall door.

She used the toilet, then sat down on it again after she'd flushed. She wanted to make sure that crazy woman was gone. Nobody in the world would hold her responsible for the end of that marriage. It might be Bob's fault or it might be Françoise's fault or it might be Alena's fault, but it certainly wasn't her fault.

She could hear the two girls at the sink murmuring to each other. They must be doing drugs of some kind, she thought. She didn't want to know what they were doing, but the little moans and groans and the occasional hiss of the faucet as it was turned on and off disturbed her, and finally she stood up, flushed again to explain her time in the stall, and stepped out.

She had to step close to the girls to wash her hands, but she tried not to look at them. In the mirror she saw that the other sink was full of bloody tissues, and she let her eyes slide sideways. The heavier girl was pressing a wad of tissue against the nose of the thin girl, who held her head way back, trying to stop the bleeding.

"Can I help?" Jen asked. "Do you need a doctor?"

It was as if she hadn't spoken. Neither of the girls answered. The heavier one dabbed at her friend's nose. The girl with the nosebleed had her eyes closed and was taking shallow breaths with her open mouth.

Jen waited, but the girls ignored her. She had the feeling that she wasn't even there. She dried her hands and crumpled the paper towel into the waste bin.

The girl with the nosebleed whimpered. The blood was gushing down her face faster than her friend could soak it up.

"I better call someone," Jen said.

"Leave us the fuck alone," the heavier girl said, glaring at Jen over her shoulder. "Mind your own business."

Jen flinched. She turned and stepped immediately back into the noisy bar. It was between sets, but everyone seemed to be shouting as if they hadn't noticed that the music had stopped. She paused and looked through the crowd. New people were sitting at the booth she had shared with Alena. It was safe to leave. She had just started toward the front of the Dream Cafe when someone called out, "Jen! Over here!"

It was Susan, a woman in her late forties with long silver hair who worked in the mailroom. She was sitting by herself at a table near the small stage. There were shirts and jackets and bags on two of the other chairs.

"Sit down," Susan grinned. "Aren't they great!" She pointed to a burly man in jeans and a faded T-shirt who was tuning a fiddle on the small stage. "That's my Ian."

Jen had heard Susan talking about her musician husband, Ian. She nodded and sat down.

"I've got something for you," Susan said. "I saw that woman you were sitting with toss these all over the floor. I thought I'd pick them up before they got trampled. Here you go. You can give them back to her. She was pretty upset, wasn't she? She'll regret she got rid of them in the morning, I know how it goes. I've been there, too."

Susan handed Jen a stack of snapshots. The top one had part of a boot heel across the sky. It showed Alena and Bob standing with their backs to a ship railing. The wind had whipped Alena's hair into her eyes. She was smiling. Bob had his arm around her waist.

"A funny thing just happened to me," Jen said. "I was at the opera looking at Marie Antoinette's harp when—"

Susan lifted her hand to stop Jen's voice. "Wait. This is my favorite, 'The Blackbird's Lament.' Listen now."

Jen listened. The tune was lively but punctuated with little riffs of sadness. She opened her purse to dump Alena's snapshots inside when she saw the two other photographs tucked into her checkbook. She'd forgotten about them.

She drew them out and looked at them. When the doctor had sent her into the other room with the optometry student to photograph her eyes, the first ones had been views taken from the wrong angle. The doctor had looked them over, then asked for another set, and he'd let Jen keep the first ones.

She'd watched them develop before her like snapshots from a Polaroid. She'd been fascinated to see the insides of her eyes. They looked like two bright orange globes. There was a small dark area on the right eye caused by the old scarring.

She placed the two squares in front of her on the table, looking at them as she listened to the music.

When the set was over, and after Susan finished applauding wildly, she turned and picked up one of the photographs.

"What in the world? What are these things, Jen? Planets? Photos of the moon?"

"These are my eyes," Jen said. "They do look like planets, don't they?"

"Really? These are eyeballs? No life on these planets, that's for sure," Susan laughed, setting the photograph back down. "You'd think looking at things would leave some kind of trace."

Jen stared at the photographs of her eyes. It was true, there was no trace of her having looked at anything. Even the scar tissue was caused by some disease she never knew she had. She had looked at things all her life, her eyeballs had recorded faces and scenes and flowers and plates of food and clouds in the sky, and none of it showed at all. Alena had been right about her. People told her things, about their sick father or their sister's miscarriage or their mother's cancer, and she'd listen and nod and say nice things, but five minutes later she would have forgotten all about their tragedies. She'd forgotten all about Marge being passed over for promotion last year. She'd forgotten to ask how her husband was doing once he got out of the hospital after the prostate operation.

"So what were you telling me, something about Marie Antoinette's harp?"

Jen nodded. She felt tired. Was she worse than other people, or the same? She had looked at that harp a few hours ago, but if they took another photograph of her eye, there wouldn't be a trace of it. But she knew what it looked like. Or did she? If someone asked her to describe it, all she could do was say the word 'harp'."

"Jen," Susan said. "Something wrong?"

Jen shook her head. "It was dark in the dungeon," she said softly, while Susan looked at her, blinking in astonishment. "Marie Antoinette couldn't see anything down there."

"What are you talking about, hon?" Susan leaned across the table.

"The harp. I'm trying to understand. I think it must have gone like this. Marie Antoinette used to play her harp in the dungeon. She'd pull it back against her and pluck the strings and try to remember a fountain tinkling at Versailles or the sound of her mother's voice. The guard out in the hall, the one who would later help her step up into the cart for the ride to the guillotine, would choke back a sob of pity and vow to himself to help her escape. But later, when he was home eating a dish of stew, he'd be so interested in his wife talking about his grandson's first step that he'd forget all about Marie Antoinette, and years afterwards, when the historians interviewed him as the last living witness of the execution, he couldn't remember the color of the dress she wore that day, and he even forgot to mention how she used to play the harp."

How to Converse
in Italian

It was a white summer night in the far, far north near the Canadian border. I'd ordered a little device from a catalogue that was supposed to imitate the wing beats of dragonflies, and scare off the mosquitoes. I didn't know if it was working, or if it was just the cool breeze up in the pines that was doing the trick, but we hadn't been bitten all night.

—My God, that year we lived up in Humboldt County still gives me a chill when I think about it, my sister said, leaning back in the lawn chair with another margarita.

—Me, too, I said.

Our husbands had gone to bed. It was just Carrie and me out on the deck. We hadn't seen each other for almost two years. My husband and I had a law office in Minneapolis, and Carrie lived in L.A. She was a writer on that long-running soap opera, *The Waves Break.* That's where she'd met her husband, Ted. He plays the brooding Olympic swimmer with amnesia—or at least he had amnesia the last time I caught one of the episodes a couple of years ago. Carrie and Ted both worked their asses off in Hollywood, and it was hard for them to get vacations together. This was the first time they'd made it up to our summer place.

Carrie and Ted had been married for eight years now. Ted never looked me in the eye, and I never could get him to talk about anything serious that was going on in the world, but I had to admit he was a hunk, and he seemed to be devoted to Carrie.

Our lives were calm and peaceful now, compared to the way we'd grown up. But sometimes, when we were alone, Carrie and I had to talk about it just to remind ourselves that those bad years had really happened, and to us.

—When I think about that house we lived in back then, Carrie said, I can't believe it. Did it really have red and black swirled carpeting and pink flowered wallpaper?

—And no central heat. You just turned on this little gas jet when it got cold, and when it felt too hot you turned it off. Mold used to grow in our shoes.

Carrie shook her head.

—That year was a turning point in our lives, she said. Dad had applied for a Guggenheim, and he said he'd take us to Italy if he got it. That's all I thought about.

—I know. Remember how we'd lie there at night talking about Italy? You especially.

—And then he really did get the Guggenheim, and instead of us all going to Italy, they got a divorce. We ended up in Daly City with Mom, and Dad moved to Provincetown with his new girlfriend.

—Well, the whole year is described in that last novel Dad wrote before he died.

Carrie finished off her margarita and leaned forward.

—But he left us out, she said, laughing a little. The couple in that novel don't have any kids. Nobody hears them fighting. God, those times they were going at it, I'd shut myself up in our room. I put in my earplugs to blur the sound, and pretend it was people I didn't know.

She looked at me. But you. You'd put your ear to the wall and listen to it all, wouldn't you?

—I just wanted to know exactly what they were fighting about so I could avoid trouble—be prepared for the next crazy thing they were likely to do.

Carrie laughed. I couldn't quite see her expression now, just the pale oval of her face in the dark.

—Listen, she said, do you remember the party to celebrate Dad's Guggenheim?

—How could I forget?

—Tell it to me. Carrie reached over and handed me my sweater from the back of another chair. Here, it's getting chilly.

—What do you mean, tell it to you?

—That's just what I mean. We've got Dad's version where the couple give a party to celebrate a winning lottery ticket, and the wife gets drunk and does a striptease on the kitchen table, but that's complete fiction. I'd like to hear your version in your own words. Then I'll tell you mine.

I laughed. If you listen to my version, that will change your version. Your memory will be contaminated.

Carrie jumped up from her chair. Just wait here a minute, she said. I'll be right back. But first I'll pour you another margarita.

—No thanks, I said.

—No thanks? But there's half a pitcher left.

—I don't want a headache tomorrow, I said. I have some briefs to go over.

I sat there in the shimmery semidark after Carrie went inside. I could smell the dew coming up through the grass below the deck. A rabbit came out of the woods, and darted under the steps that led down to the lawn. I thought about Carrie and me and how we were both different and the same. She had finally cut her long blond hair. Now that she was in her thirties, her cheekbones were more prominent, and she looked so exactly like Mom that I had gasped when I met her and Ted at the airport. She had the same flashing, steel-blue eyes. I took after Dad. I had dark hair and had to watch my weight, and if I drank anything—even a couple of glasses of wine—I got these deep pouches under my eyes that frightened me. I'd see Dad's face staring back at me from the mirror, and I'd go for weeks at a time afraid to even have one beer.

After Mom got married again to a jerk of a high-school football coach, Carrie won a scholarship to UCLA and took off. I didn't have the money to live away from home while I went to college, so I moved in with my grandmother in Minneapolis and went to the University of Minnesota. That's where I met Barry. We got married the day that Dad killed himself in a one-car accident as he drove back to Provincetown from Boston. Barry and I went to law school together, and when we passed our bar exams, we opened a joint practice which did pretty well. Three years ago we built this house up north so we'd have someplace to get away to on weekends.

Carrie slid back the screen door and came back out. She had a sheaf of paper in one hand.

—What's that? I asked.

—I'm writing a memoir. It's Ted's idea. Everyone's writing memoirs now, and since Dad is famous—anyway, this is the section about the party. I'll read it to you, but first I want to hear you tell about it.

I looked at her doubtfully.

—Please, she said. Tell me everything you remember about the party and everything leading up to it.

—My God, Carrie, I laughed. Everything leading up to it? I'd have to start with being born. I'd have to tell about growing up in that trailer in Portland and then that miserable year in Chico where they tried home schooling and then how about that awful summer when they ran the tourist camp in Montana?

—No, she said, I mean just tell about that last year in California.

—But where do I start?

—Start with the weather, she said. That's always a good place to begin.

.   .   .

So I started.

—The day we drove into Eureka the temperature was 55 degrees, I said, and the day we drove out the next June it was 55 degrees. And in between it mostly stayed 55 degrees. It was foggy when it wasn't raining, and on rare sunny days a stiff wind off the ocean would blow the smell of the paper mill all over town.

Dad had an advance for a novel. It wasn't as big as his agent promised, but it was almost enough to live on for a year, and since Mom hated her government job, they decided to try for a new life. Dad knew someone who had an empty, furnished house for rent up in Humboldt County, the end of the world, he said, no distractions, you can just smell the sea air and walk in the redwoods and smoke the best shit in the world and write the great American novel, and Mom could pick up a part-time job somewhere, and we girls could go to high school and everything would be great while Dad wrote the book. And if he got the grant he'd put in for, we'd all go to Italy next year and learn Italian and eat pasta.

I listened to them talking up the idea. We'd live in this big house by the sea, like in that old movie we saw on TV one night, *The Ghost and Mrs. Muir*. We'd go clamming on the beach, and Dad could look out at the view while he wrote, and Mom could find agates and make rings and sell them to shops in town.

It sounded too good to be true, so I wasn't surprised when we pulled up to this little two-bedroom bungalow on a narrow street crowded with lots of other bungalows that looked just like it, some with rusting junk or old beaters of cars in the yards, and the yards all weeds and unmowed grass, except for the poor widow next door who had to go out on Sunday mornings to pick beer bottles out of her flower beds. Mom started to cry, sitting there in the car. She wouldn't even open the door. Dad had to go around and open it for her. It was the usual pattern—oh, honey, it'll be all right, you'll see, we'll make this place into a real home, blah, blah, blah, while Mom kept crying and finally he started shouting at her. That was what she was waiting for. She shouted back. Remember, Carrie? You and me were cringing in the back seat.

Months went by—cold, gloomy, miserable months. I swear I never took off that down vest I wore, even inside. We seldom saw Mom and Dad at breakfast because their hangovers kept them in bed, and when I got home from school, in the rain, it was almost dark and they'd already be shaking a pitcher of martinis. And then later, when Mom was on the wagon, she'd get up early some mornings and sit there smoking while we ate our Cheerios, sometimes complaining about the damp house, but other times just talking about the old days when she and Dad were both young and just starting out. They'd gone to Italy on their honeymoon. It was the year they'd both graduated from college, and Europe was cheap. She'd describe these three-course lunches with wine at outdoor restaurants that cost 80 cents, and how they'd walk around Venice in a daze, leaning over bridges or looking up at gilded buildings, pinching themselves so they'd know they weren't dreaming. But sometimes Dad had stayed up all night writing, and he'd get us to fry him an egg. He'd go on about Italy, too. He'd tell us about how great things were going to be next year. We'd find an apartment in a Renaissance palace and Italian boys would whistle at us because we were such good-looking girls.

I got home from school one February afternoon, and as I was shaking out my umbrella on the front stoop, Mom opened the door and her face was lit up. She hugged me, wet coat and all, and shouted that we really were going to Italy.

They'd called Dad from New York. He'd won a Guggenheim.

Dad had this record. It was called "Hear How to Converse in Italian," and he'd gotten it free from Alitalia Airlines one time. He put it on our old K-Mart stereo that night, and we all sat around repeating the phrases. *La carta, prègo,* Dad would repeat, then it was my turn and I'd shout out *Quanto costa* and you'd yell *Che dolci avete* or something like that. We went through the whole record saying funny things in Italian like *Are there any operas scheduled tonight?* or *Where is the shopping district in this city?* We were all laughing and interrupting each other and Mom was snuggled up against Dad and they'd told us we didn't have to do our homework and it seemed to me that this time it was all going to work out—Dad wasn't just talking big about getting a grant for Italy, he really had one, and we were really going to go.

That was the last time I remember being happy together as a family.

Mom and Dad decided to throw a party that weekend. Dad had fans at the local college and he knew the bookstore people, and Mom knew people at the craft store where she worked part-time. They ordered a cake shaped like a gondola, a couple of big lasagnas from a caterer, eggplant dip and bread sticks and olives and all kinds of other stuff I can't remember. Mom had bright spots of color in her cheeks, and Dad was beaming and smiling as they unpacked groceries, and he kept grabbing her around the waist and kissing her neck and saying *Prègo* or *Benissimo.*

The only problem was, Mom was still on the wagon. She was going out to AA meetings twice a week, and she was determined she was going to stick it out this time. She was happy to provide a lot of drinks for the guests, she said, but as for herself, she was only going to drink cranberry juice.

—Well, OK, Dad said, but we *are* going to Italy. In Italy everyone drinks wine.

—Fine, Mom said. But we're not in Italy now.

At first it seemed like the old pattern starting up again. Going on the wagon was a way one of them could punish the other after a big blowup. When they were both drinking, they were happy and they'd talk wildly and make these big plans. They'd be excited and sweet to one another for weeks, nursing each other's hangovers. But then things would start building up, Dad's agent would give him some bad news, or Mom's boss would hassle her at work, or the car would break down again, and you'd feel the tension. They'd start snapping at each other or at us, and finally one night they'd really go at it. Those were the nights you'd put in your earplugs and cover your head with a pillow. But I'd sit there with my back against our bedroom door, holding the iron skillet in my lap in case they started beating each other up. I wanted to be ready to get past them and call the police.

But this time, Mom really wanted to stay sober. Usually it was good news that made her drink, so I was expecting her to give in to her joy about going to Italy and have a glass of Chianti when Dad opened the straw-covered bottle at dinner the night before the party. But she wouldn't. The conversation went something like this:

—Jesus, Diane. Are you going to sit around drinking milk in the Piazza San Marco?

—Honey, don't do this to me. I'm trying to fight an addiction. Please help me, OK?

—But everyone drinks wine in Italy. Even children drink wine in Italy. Carrie, Leslie, bring a couple of more glasses. I want you girls to get used to drinking wine with your meals.

—Don't you dare. Don't you dare pour my daughters a glass of wine.

—For Christ's sake, honey! Not even mixed with mineral water? Do you want a couple of stiff little American namby-pambys? They'll be laughingstocks.

—Carrie, put that glass back on the shelf! Do you hear me?

So that was the day before the party. They smoothed it over, but later that night Dad had this bottle of Amaretto he'd bought, and while we were in the kitchen together doing the dishes, he gave me a sip. I didn't especially want to taste the stuff—it tasted awful, actually—but I knew that if I refused he'd be pissed and get irritable, and that if I sipped some, he'd be pleased that he'd done something behind Mom's back, and he'd be cheerful all evening. But later I wished I'd said no.

So now we come to the party. I remember that same dark misty rain was falling. I could see the whole living room reflected in the picture window, and the house looked twice as large, even spacious with all Dad's friends milling about holding beer bottles or paper cups of wine. But when they started to pass a joint around, Mom pulled the curtains shut, and the room got small and stuffy and everyone started talking louder and louder. Once I collected a bag full of empty bottles, and I took it outside in the backyard just to get some fresh air. Remember the apple trees back there? The rotten apples were still on the ground, and the grass was thick and wet. I walked around in the dark, smushing apples under my shoes. They had an ancient, rotten smell. I pretended there was a canal out there just beyond the fence, instead of an alley, and that gondolas were floating past in the dark.

I went back inside. That's when it happened. I don't know where the bottle of Asti Spumante came from. Anyway, Dad had just opened it and he wanted to make a toast to Italy. He'd gotten one of the crystal champagne flutes out of the cabinet, and he'd poured Mom a glass. They were both standing in a circle of people, but she wouldn't take the glass.

—Please, honey, I'm not drinking, she said, and her mouth was thin and tight. She had her arms crossed.

—It's a toast to Italy, Dad insisted. His face was gleaming and his eyes were bright from drinking all night.

—I don't care if it's a toast to the pope and the whole goddamn college of cardinals, Mom said, and everyone laughed.

—Jesus, you're a hard woman. And that's when he spotted me.

—Here, Leslie, he said. You toast your old man. To Italy.

And he thrust the glass into my hand.

Mom had turned white. Don't drink it, Leslie, she said in a shaking voice.

—Leslie's not ashamed to have a drink with her old man, are you, baby? Dad grinned at me. *Posso offrirle un aperitivo?* he said.

—You want to hear how to converse in Italian? Mom raised her arm. She made a gesture.

Dad's eyes got slitty. Some of the guests—those who were still sober enough to recognize what was going on—slipped away, and somebody turned up the volume on the stereo. The three of us stood there looking at each other, me holding this frothing glass of bubbles, which would have been the first glass of sparkling wine I'd ever tasted in my life if I'd drunk it, and Mom and Dad looking at each other with such hatred that I wanted to sink down through the floor, just disappear through a trap door in a cloud of stage fog, and get out of their theatrical lives forever.

We all knew what was going to happen, and none of us did anything to stop it. I stood there holding the glass until Dad took it out of my hand, and Mom stood there daring him with her eyes, and Dad knew we were both waiting for him to go through with it. So he did. He flung the Asti Spumante into Mom's face and hurled the glass down on that awful red and black carpet. The glass didn't break. Dad smashed it with his shoe while Mom shrieked and wiped her eyes. Then she leapt on him and began tearing at his hair.

People pulled them apart. The party broke up. I sat against the bedroom door holding the skillet, sick to my stomach. The things they said to each other that night still give me the shudders, Carrie.

.   .   .

Carrie had a funny look on her face. She handed me some sheets of paper. I moved my chair into the shaft of light coming out from the sliding door to the kitchen, and started to read from her memoir.

In that vanished time, I read, when we lived by the Pacific Ocean, my father used to pick me up at the high school after he'd finished his day's writing. Seniors started earlier and were dismissed earlier than the other classes (most seniors had after-school jobs), and I could have waited in study hall and come home on the bus with my sister. But when my father started picking me up in our old battered Aspen station wagon, I was delighted. I'd toss my books on top of the clutter of jackets and Coke cans and newspapers in the back, and slide onto the front seat beside him, ready to go anywhere he wanted.

At first he liked to take walks with me to clear his head. We'd walk through the town's redwood forest, down a ravine through thick wet ferns as tall as ordinary trees. But the big redwoods, looming up into the fog, depressed him. They made him feel like he was the size of an ant, he said, and so for a few weeks we drove out to Clam Beach and walked by the ocean. But in the winter there were always storms out there, and we'd have to stand far back from the shore, wary of waves as tall as rooftops, watching huge logs wash in, logs that must have floated all the way down from Oregon.

So we started going to Silvio's.

Silvio's was a windowless cinderblock tavern with a weedy parking lot full of rusted cars with big fins. It had a tall, rusting, rectangular sign that said SILVIO'S. Below it was the neon outline of a cocktail glass, and another sign that said COCK AILS. The first time we drove there, a banner made from a sheet was hanging down from the roof that said:

In Loving Memory of "Rowdy" Henderson
OUR FRIEND

My father told me that Rowdy had been one of the regulars at the tavern. He'd died suddenly of a heart attack.

That first afternoon at Silvio's we sat at a table in the corner. My father had a draft and a cigarette, and I had a Coke with two cherries stuck on a swizzle stick. At first it was quiet. A few old men were sitting on stools at the bar when we first got there, talking in low voices; but toward quitting time men in workboots and plaid shirts, and a few women in polyester pants suits began to drop by, and the tables filled up. By the time we left, the place was hazy with cigarette smoke and noisy with talk. That first time, my father drove home, but when we stopped at Silvio's again the next afternoon, he had two drafts and a shot of whiskey. I'd recently gotten my license, so he let me drive. And after that it became customary. My father would drink as much as he wanted, and I'd drive us home. My mother worked in the afternoons, so she knew nothing about Silvio's. By the time she got back to the house, my father already had a drink in his hand, and she was allowed to assume it was his first of the evening.

I liked going to Silvio's. I was proud of my father because he was so popular, and I thought that my mother and sister did not fully appreciate him. At Silvio's, he always had this pleasant, relaxed expression on his face. He seemed to know everyone, and it was clear that everyone liked him. Both men and women stopped by our table to say hello, and someone always pulled up a chair and chatted awhile. They'd go on about the salmon fishing, or complain about something the lumber company had just announced, or confide how their daughter down in Sacramento had just been diagnosed with MS, or else they'd give out general advice about the best place in town to get a brake job or buy crabs or pawn a ring. My father listened respectfully to everything. He seemed interested in people's lives, and I was amazed by the things people confided to him while I sat there sipping my Coke.

We stopped at Silvio's a couple of days after my father had gotten the Guggenheim. Word had gone around that he'd won money to go to Italy, and people came over to shake his hand or slap him on the back. And everyone wanted to buy him a drink.

Then this little incident happened. It was a thing that brought out the best side of my father's character, and made me sure that we were going to have a happy time in Italy. My father had a gift for making friends, and I imagined us sitting in an outdoor cafe surrounded by handsome men and women speaking Italian.

Two little blond boys were running around Silvio's that afternoon. One must have been three or so, and the other about five. Their young father, who looked barely out of his teens, was having a beer at the bar, and every now and then, when they got too rambunctious, and started giggling or crawling under tables, he'd get up, and in a pleasant way herd them both back to a table in the corner to finish their Cokes.

I had a good view of the outside door. Whenever anyone pushed it open, they'd always pause for a moment on this scrap of muddy carpet until their eyes adjusted to the dimness. Then they either spotted a friend, or picked out an empty table or a place at the bar. I played this game where I'd guess whether the person coming in knew anyone in Silvio's or not. If they were regulars, they'd look around boldly, but if they were newcomers, they'd dart furtive glances around the room, and make a quick dash for a chair or stool.

That afternoon a young woman came through the door. Her hair had just been permed, and I could smell the solution. She reached up and patted the back of her head as her eyes adjusted. Then she spotted the little boys.

"Eddie! Billie!" she cried. She looked wildly around the room until she found their father. She ran over to the bar.

"Oh, Jesus, Howard. The barber said he hadn't seen you. So this is where you bring them for haircuts!"

The young father slid off his stool, pushing his beer glass away, turning red. The whole room had quieted, and everyone was watching.

"You've just spent their haircut money on beer, haven't you? Oh, Jesus, Howard, how could you!" The young woman buried her face in her hands. She began to shake with sobs, while the two boys stood looking up at her, and the husband looked at his shoes.

"I'm sorry, honey," he murmured.

"Sorry!" She dropped her hands and looked at him. "That's the last money until next payday. And look at them. Look at them."

She grabbed one of the boys by the shoulders and thrust him forward.

"You're just an old drunk, Howard. You're twenty-two and you're an old drunk already. What kind of future are they going to have, I ask you? I ask you, Howard?"

The young father hunched his shoulders. He did not look at her.

That's when my father came to the rescue.

He stood up, and stepped over toward the couple. He had this warm, kindly look on his face.

"Howard, looks like we better get started on those haircuts. I'm sorry, Ma'am," he added, turning to the young woman. "I told your husband I'd cut the boys' hair if he brought them by here, and then I got to talking, and the time just flew."

My father turned to the bartender. "Joe, give me that pair of scissors in the drawer back there, and hand me one of those towels, will you?"

Then my father reached down, grabbed one of the little blond boys, and plopped him on a bar stool.

"Hold still now, son," he said, and the boy just blinked up at him. He draped the bar towel around the boy's shoulders, pulled a comb out of his back pocket, and picked up the scissors the bartender had placed on the bar. Then he proceeded to cut the boys' hair, just the way he used to cut our hair, and sometimes even mother's hair, to save money. Little licks of blond hair fell around the boy's shoulders, and mixed in with the popcorn on the floor, and everyone in the bar watched in almost complete silence.

"Next," he said. And he cut the hair of the other little boy.

The young couple stood there, not looking at each other and not saying anything. Then the woman took the two boys by the hand. She looked at my father. "Thank you," she said in a low voice. "Let's go, Howard."

Howard reached out and shook my father's hand. "I won't forget this," he said in a low voice as his wife headed for the door. "I owe you and I won't forget."

When the door shut on the couple, a big cheer went up for my father. My face got red and hot. I was so proud of him for saving the situation. I think everyone in the place must have tried to pat him on the back, and of course they all wanted to know how he'd learned to cut hair like that. "Necessity," was all he'd say, grinning, and his modesty made everyone like him even more.

On the way home that afternoon, my father and I tried talking only in Italian. We shouted and laughed and made up new Italian words to go with the handful we knew, and as I looked through the misted windshield, the green fields dotted with cows and egrets disappeared, and it was the turquoise Adriatic that I was driving beside, and those towers in the distance weren't the smokestacks of the pulp mill, they were the dreamlike campanile of Venice.

And my happiness lasted on through the party my parents gave that weekend to celebrate my father's Guggenheim.

Every time I ate one of those oil-soaked olives, or cut a piece of Fontina cheese, or took a bite of the lasagna, I imagined eating such food at an outdoor cafe in Florence, looking up at golden Renaissance facades. And when Mitch Kirkwood, the owner of Uranina Books, showed me the bottle of Asti Spumante he'd brought, and asked me if I could find a couple of champagne glasses—real glasses, not paper cups—so he could pour a toast for my parents, I went eagerly to the cabinet in the kitchen, and rinsed off two dusty champagne flutes in the sink, not considering the fact that my mother wasn't drinking at the party, because this had nothing to do with drinking, I foolishly thought, it had to with dreams, and if I had been my mother, I would have drunk such a toast. And later when she refused, and when Dad gave her glass to my sister, Leslie, and Leslie just stood there confused by their conflicting commands, one telling her to drink, and the other ordering her not to, I reached out to grab the glass from her hand. I was going to drink it, but I was a second too late. My father grabbed the glass back from my sister, and flung the contents into my mother's face.

And that was the end of everything.

·   ·   ·

I looked over at my sister, who had moved one of the lounge chairs away from the shaft of kitchen light to the far edge of the deck. She was lying back, sipping a margarita, looking up at the night sky. I wondered if she could see the stars, or if the light I was using to read by hazed her view.

—Do you really think everything would have been different if you'd grabbed that glass before he did?

Carrie didn't say anything.

—Don't you think they would have just found something else to fight about?

I heard the lounger creak as she pulled up her legs.

—Is that what you think, Leslie? That we were just fated not to go to Italy?

—You and Ted went to Italy, didn't you? A couple of years ago? I'm the one who's never been to Europe.

—We went for a week, Carrie said. One week. That's all the time we had. I had to write Ted's character into a body cast so someone else could play him for a few episodes.

—But it was Italy, wasn't it?

—It wasn't the same, she said. That's not what I'm talking about, Leslie. I'm talking about when I was seventeen.

Something buzzed my face. It might have been a mosquito, after all.

—Well, I said. I'd rather think that there were a lot of factors involved in what happened to Mom and Dad—the whole history of their marriage, their addictions, particular circumstances, their genes even.

Carrie swung her legs down on the deck. No, she said. If I'd only been one second quicker, I'd have grabbed that glass. I'd have drunk that stuff, and we would have all gone to Italy. I'd speak Italian now.

I sighed. I shuffled the sheets of paper in my hand. I tried to remember what it felt like to stand there holding that champagne flute all those years ago. I'd felt paralyzed. I'd made no move to put it to my lips. I didn't want to humiliate Mom in public, but if I had gone ahead and poured it down the way Dad wanted me to, would I have saved their marriage? Would we have gone to Italy and lived happily ever after? Would Dad still be alive? I didn't think so.

Carrie was standing at the rail of the deck, looking out at the dark yard, her back to me.

—I'm happy, she said. I love Ted. I love my work. But sometimes I catch glimpses—or maybe it's like hearing whispers in another language—of this other life I might have led. It almost seems to exist, to be floating out there like an invisible ship. Sometimes it moves in close, and just hovers there, as if it's waiting for me to swim out and climb on board.

I stepped up beside her. The night odors were rising, the secret perfumes of birch leaves and mushrooms and night-crawlers and pine boughs, which might have been floating in from some invisible island out there in the dark. One tall pine stood in faint relief against the horizon, like a ship's mast.

—How do you say "Isn't it a beautiful night?" in Italian, I asked.

—I'm sorry, Carrie said. I don't know how to converse in Italian.

The Cliffs of the Moon

Early evening. The moon has not yet risen, and the far range of mountains, with the Matterhorn looming up like a big seashell, is drowned in rose light. You can see a whole little village on a ledge across the valley, complete with church steeple and outlying cowsheds. Down below, the valley is already dark, and lights twinkle here and there, first two or three, then a few more, then dozens, until the whole length of the town of Sierre glitters in outline. Yet the sky is transparent when you look straight up, like the inside of a newly washed mixing bowl.

On most of the balconies of the Residence des Alpes, the striped canvas chairs have been folded, and placed on their sides. The sliding-glass windows on the rez-de-chaussée are dark, but on the premier étage, the middle apartment is brightly lit, the filmy curtains not yet drawn. A honeymoon couple sit at a table just inside, looking out at the view. Up on the deuxième étage, a balding man with a mustache is leaning over the railing. Indistinct jazz wafts out of the half-open door behind him. On the balcony next to the man, but blocked from his sight by a privacy wall, a woman with iron-grey hair appears with a watering can. She drenches the roots of each geranium in the planter attached to the railing.

A brilliant, amorphous light strikes just behind the rim of the mountains. The sky turns bluer, and darker. Then, as if cranked up by some kind of fantastic machine, the curving top of the moon appears.

The woman stops watering in amazement, holding her can in midair. Higher and higher the moon rises, so enormous and so pulsing with radiance that it seems to be at first a doorway to somewhere, an entrance cut into the sky, rather than a planet. The honeymoon couple get up from their table, and each taking a wine glass, step outside, arms touching. The wife sips her white wine, tasting the color in her throat. Her husband feels a silvery spark on his lips when he kisses her neck. The man listening to jazz above them shudders and scratches his ear, as if he might hear the moon's rhythm if he could only shake some obstruction out of his head.

.   .   .

The moon seems to shrink as it rises higher in the sky. Ellen can see the spots across it, shadows of mountains, depressions, the looming cliffs and the plains mapped by astronauts. She sets down the watering can and steps back inside. Her manuscript pages are scattered over the little table in front of the window. She snatches up the chapter of the biography she's been working on all day. She's trying to conjure Katherine Mansfield. But how dry and brittle her words seem as she reads them over. The moon isn't in them. The geraniums are missing. There's no smell of pine.

That morning she'd gone down in the funicular to look for Rilke's house, and gotten off at the wrong stop, in the middle of vineyards. She'd panicked when she looked up and saw nothing but terraces of twisted vines halfway up the mountainside. Below her the roofs of Sierre had disappeared. The sun blazed down. She felt thirsty and out of breath, and the flies buzzed around her face, attracted by her sweat. Finally she'd spotted a shirtless farmer, and he'd directed her down the right row of vines, where she came to a service road, and found one of the familiar yellow Swiss signposts. Château Muzot was closed to visitors, so she'd stood outside the gate, looking at the stone tower where Rilke had written the last elegies and the sonnets to Orpheus. Of course he knew nothing of the woman dying and struggling to write up in the village of Montana above him. If he'd ever passed her, maybe on the platform of the railway station in the summer of 1921, he would have seen only another feverish consumptive.

A moth has flown inside, and is fluttering wildly around the bulb of the swag lamp over the table. She switches it off, then slides back the door to the balcony again. The moon seems as bright as a spotlight, and she waits for the moth to fly straight toward it. A sweet odor of tobacco wafts in with the breeze, and she thinks of Evan, her husband, stepping outside for a smoke every night after supper, even after he'd been diagnosed with lung cancer.

.   .   .

Philippe hears his neighbor's balcony door open, and stubs out his cigarette in the planter. Americans don't like smoke. He doesn't want to bother her. She seems to be short of breath. He's heard her wheezing on the stairs.

He leans over the railing, thinking he hears his wife's car, but it must be someone on the way down to the vacation colony at Moubra. He remembers seeing a moon like this the first time he rented a place up here above the Rhône valley. It was a cold night in June. He and his daughter, Marguerite, had paused outside the Halle de Glace in the center of the village of Montana, watching the skaters through the big window. Most of them were teenagers in cut-off jeans and sweatshirts, energetically awkward, but one slim blond girl in leotards twirled by herself in the center of the ice, her hair flying out as she gracefully lifted first one leg and then the other, her silver blades flashing. The others eyed her over their shoulders, clumsily attempting to mock her swirls and pirouettes. Her eyes were half-closed. She didn't notice the other skaters tumbling and giggling and showing off around her. She was concentrating only on the perfection of her movements.

Without thinking, he had exclaimed, "How beautifully that girl skates!"

Marguerite had jerked back, and started down the Allée Katherine Mansfield toward the lake, dragging her left leg. She'd been in the car with her grandfather when a truck had slid into their path on a slippery mountain road when she was fifteen. Her grandfather—Philippe's father—had managed to veer away just in time, but they'd slammed into a concrete embankment. He'd been killed instantly. Marguerite had broken both her legs and crushed the bones in her feet. She'd dreamed of being an Olympic skier before the accident.

Philippe caught up with her. She'd stopped abruptly, her face in her hands. He took her arm and made her sit down on one of the red benches that faced the valley.

"Do you want a pill?"

She shook her head. She began to take deep breaths, the way she'd been taught.

Then the moon had risen. Dazzling white, enormous, unreal, it seemed to be so close that surely it was going to float straight across the valley. The light bathed Marguerite's face. He might have forgotten the moon that evening except that, just then, Marguerite had stretched out her arms as if she could reach up and grab handfuls of its milky crust. "If I lived up there," she said, "I could jump off a cliff and it wouldn't hurt."

Tonight's moon had come up like that. But just like the moon of years ago, it wasn't floating straight across the valley. It was climbing and climbing, and the darkness was thickening on the earth. He remembered how he had put his arm around Marguerite that time, feeling as miserable and as helpless as he did at his job in Geneva when he had to translate some new atrocity into French.

Now he sees a car entering the lot below. The headlights blind him for a moment. His wife gets out first, pausing for a moment by the door to hand Marguerite her cane.

.   .   .

Lotte guesses it must be cold, but she's been out here drinking glasses of moonlight, and she's hardly noticed. But there are goose pimples on her bare arms. No, she doesn't want her sweater. More wine, please. Peter slips back into the dark apartment just as a car pulls into the lot. Headlights flash up, and she feels herself momentarily illuminated. Then the car backs into one of the empty parking spaces. Two women get out stiffly, one leaning on a cane.

She watches the women cross the dark lot. The older one, her head tucked down, heads straight for the lobby entrance. The younger one, limping with her cane, stops for a moment and stares up at the moon. The light illuminates her broad, pale face and the bobbing motion of her throat. She seems to be swallowing tears. Her dark hair, frizzy at the ends, floats back over her collar.

Peter comes back out with the bottle. "Look," he says, "mist is rising up from the valley."

The woman below hears his voice. She glances up, looking directly into Lotte's eyes for a moment, then brusquely moves after the older woman, who must be holding the lobby door open for her, as there is now a rectangle of pale light spread across the walk below.

"Peter," Lotte murmurs, "did you see that woman?"

"What about her?"

"She looked so sad."

"You're always trying to imagine what other people feel. It's not a good idea, Lotte."

"I know."

He kisses her on the neck. "*You* aren't sad, are you?"

"No, of course not."

And she isn't sad, not anymore. That gloomy feeling she'd had yesterday in Regensberg when she first came out on the steps of the thirteenth-century church in her white dress, and her friends and her parents' friends had crowded around to throw rice and streamers, bumping against her so that she'd stumbled in her satin shoes on the cobblestones, that feeling that her life was a bubble, and that she was as transient as the white roses in her bouquet, picked, dethorned, already dead although their soft petals still smelled sweet, that feeling had been caused by the long service, her empty stomach, the pain of kneeling on marble steps before the altar, her mother's tense voice, the razor cut on Peter's neck (couldn't he shave properly on his wedding day!), her father's gloating eyes, and the slobbering kisses and squeezes of his banker colleagues, who seemed to feel they had a right to fondle her. She had felt the prick of a pin in the chaplet of flowers arranged on her head, had sighed at the thought of the elaborate wedding dinner in the garden of the Restaurant Bellevue she'd have to sit through, the long, sentimental toasts, and had been annoyed by the group of Australian tourists photographing her from across the street as if she were a "quaint" attraction like the half-timbered burghers' houses. But the drive across the mountains with Peter (everyone thought they'd gone down to Lugano to swim), had calmed and cured her completely. She'd regained her happiness in the dark car. And now, tonight, this full moon rising up over the Valais Alps.

Peter slips his hands up under her T-shirt. His fingers are cold from holding the wine bottle, and she gasps with pleasure as he begins to knead her breasts. She leans back against him, her nipples hard, and closes her eyes.

Why shouldn't she try to be happy? Why shouldn't she just give into it and admit that she is one of the lucky people in the world?

Suddenly Peter drops his hands. "I left our bread in the car," he says. "I'll be right back."

.   .   .

As Marguerite pours Bordeaux into three glasses, she notices herself reflected in the wall of glass windows. She smiles, and her other self smiles back. If only the other self were the one who did things first. Then she would leap into the air, and Marguerite would leap into the air, too.

She sets the bottle back on the table, slides open the balcony door, and steps outside. People are always taking sun baths, so why not moon baths? She looks up at the round bright light. If she were alone, she'd take off all her clothes and stretch out in one of the canvas chairs.

That woman she'd glimpsed from the parking lot reminded her so much of Fanchette. She had the same short bangs and wide high cheekbones. She thinks of Fanchette's last letter, still in her handbag, creased and wrinkled from so many rereadings. How strange to think that she'll never see Fanchette again, never again kiss those lips that always tasted of cocoa butter, or put her arms around those freckled, sandy shoulders. She'd always sensed something mocking and elusive in Fanchette's deep blue eyes, had seen her staring boldly at the breasts of other women on the beach, and had felt her attention wandering off even when Marguerite clung tightly to her hand when they walked out to the headland above the beach at St.-Jean-de-Luz to make out in the hydrangea bushes, but she'd always thought she could keep her by the fierceness of her lovemaking, and create an addiction to a mouth willing to suck tenderly or violently at every part of her body.

But Fanchette has met a rock singer in Paris with gold rings through her nipples. She's not coming to St.-Jean-de-Luz this August.

Marguerite can feel the bitterness carving lines into the tender skin around her mouth. She fears that she's starting to look older than her age. She closes her eyes, imagining the moonlight filling her pores like a magic lotion.

Her father raps on the glass.

She steps back into the apartment. "Did you see the moon tonight, Papa?"

"Spectacular," he says, carefully bringing a bowl of soup to the table. "When I was a boy, I thought we'd be making regular space flights to the moon—it would be just like flying to New York."

"It's too bad. Only astronauts have been up there."

"Now I know they'd only turn it into a penal colony," he says. "If there were cheap flights to the moon, thousands—maybe hundreds of thousands—of people would be imprisoned up there. Those shadows you see would be the camps."

Marguerite looks away from him. She and her mother have been trying to get Papa to retire early. He's been complaining that he can't get the voices out of his head anymore—the testimonies, the pleas for help, the descriptions of massacres that he has to find words for every day. At least he's out of it for this bit of holiday. She wishes she could go on a long hike with him up to the glacier. If he wore himself out physically, she thinks, the voices might stop and he'd be able to sleep.

She reaches behind her and turns up the volume on the CD player. Jazz helps him relax.

Her mother bustles into the kitchen. "How wonderful it smells, Philippe."

"Soupe d'avoine," he says. "Sit down, my dear. Tell me what the new doctor said."

"He suggested the thermal baths at Aix-les-Bains." She does not look at Marguerite.

Marguerite clanks her soupspoon against the bowl. "Thermal baths are fine as long as you stay in the water," she says. "If I were a mermaid I could turn somersaults all day."

. . .

The music from the apartment next door drifts through Ellen's open window, a little louder than before. She concentrates. That melody is so familiar. Then she recognizes the opening phrase of the clarinet solo. It's Sidney Bechet playing the "Weary Blues," one of Evan's favorite pieces.

When he was diagnosed with lung cancer, it seemed to confirm something he already knew, as if he'd been reassured to see evidence that his life was nothing at all. He'd sit in the living room after supper, listening to his collection of old records for hours at a time. Ellen had been frightened by his depression as much as she was by the fear of losing him. He wouldn't let her touch him the night before the first chemo treatment began. She'd waited for him to fall into a troubled sleep, and then she put her arms around him and clung to his bony body as if she were drowning.

Ellen turns up the burner on the stove. She's cooking a pizza in the skillet with a pie tin as a lid. At first she'd been annoyed to discover that her efficiency had no oven, but then she'd discovered she could cook frozen quiche and pizza just as well on the electric plates. She's almost lost her appetite since Evan's death. She has to force herself to make even a salad. She's lost ten pounds in the last six months.

The clarinet draws her out on the balcony again. She listens to "Mood Indigo." The moon is bright and high in the sky, but she's surprised to see that the whole broad valley below has disappeared in a thick white cloud, which laps at the tips of the pines on the steep slope below the apartment building. It's like finding yourself in another world, she thinks. Or perhaps she's dead, and this is the view from heaven, cloud after cloud obscuring the meaning of everything on earth, so that only pure forms are left, the shapes of planets and their moons and the essence of light.

At the time Evan died she'd already finished the research for her biography, and completed most of the first draft. It seemed like a good idea to get away from her grief, and come to this place in Switzerland where Katherine Mansfield had written some of her greatest stories while dying of tuberculosis. The change might inspire her, and the landscape might give her some insight into her subject's character, or at least distract her a little from her own depression. But now she's beginning to doubt everything she's written. She feels like a medium pretending to call up a ghost at a séance.

And she keeps thinking about Evan, too. What if she herself, knowing and loving him so well, tried to reconstruct Evan? Reconstruct his appearance from photographs that are gradually replacing her memory, his voice from a tape recording, his thoughts from remembered conversations and letters friends might have saved by chance, his mind from the bibliography in the back of his book on Chaucer, his interests by cataloging the number of Sidney Bechet albums in his jazz collection, his boyhood from his brother's jealous anecdotes, his early love life from an old girlfriend's resentments—how ridiculous to think she can even come close to Evan, she who slept beside him for twenty-eight years.

And Katherine Mansfield has been dead for over seventy years.

She draws a bitter gust of smoke into her mouth. She coughs. What in the world? Then she turns to see a black cloud pouring out the open door behind her.

.   .   .

Peter runs up the stairs, baguette in hand. Then he stops suddenly on the landing. Smoke rolls down from the floor above.

His heart bangs convulsively in his chest. For a second he's six again, trying to wake up his sleeping brother as smoke pours out from under the sill of the door. Foolishly he had opened the door to a wall of flames and heat, which drove him screaming to the window. He had crawled out onto the ledge of the apartment building.

Shuddering, trying not to think, he forces himself to run up into the smoke just as the alarm in the hall goes off with a piercing shriek.

The door of one of the apartments on the floor above is wide open. Smoke is billowing out, but through the gusts he glimpses a grey-haired woman who seems to be flapping at it with a wet dish towel. Then the door of another apartment bursts open. A man in shorts begins shouting in French, directing two women, who have crowded to the door behind him, to get back inside the apartment. He slams the door on them.

Down on the floor below, Peter hears Lotte screaming his name. The alarm blasts his eardrums.

"The fire's out," the woman with the dish towel yells in English as Peter plunges toward her. "I'm trying to get rid of the smoke."

He steps through the door of the woman's apartment, waving the baguette to clear the grey haze from his face. A funnel of thick smoke coils up from a skillet in the sink. Water from the tap sizzles over it, soaking some blackened thing that had been cooking there. He feels faint.

"My pizza caught fire," the woman gasps.

Across the single large room, Peter sees that the sliding-glass doors are wide open. Some of the smoke is blowing out that way.

The woman bends over, coughing and choking. Peter grabs her arm and leads her out to the balcony.

"Breathe deep," he says, pushing her to the railing. The moon is veiled by the drifting smoke as it dissipates into the night air. He's back with the firemen on the square in Basel. Someone has put a blanket around his shoulders. They're turning him away, but not before he glimpses his brother's charred body on the stretcher. His head looks like that thing in the skillet.

"What happened?" The man from next door has joined them on the balcony. He speaks perfect English.

"She was cooking. It caught fire."

"Is she all right?"

"I'm fine," the woman sobs, pressing her chest. Her face is flushed.

"Papa, what is it?" A young woman is peering around the privacy wall.

"It's all right, my dear. Just a small cooking fire."

"I'm so sorry," the grey-haired woman says. "I got distracted, I was thinking about something, and then all at once I smelled the smoke." She looks as if she might collapse.

Peter looks at the older man.

"You can't stay here. This place must be aired out," he says to the woman. "Please come next door. We're just having dinner."

"I'll turn off the alarm," Peter says, taking a chair out in the hall to stand on.

Downstairs, Lotte is waiting outside their apartment. He feels like shaking her.

"You shouldn't have come out in the hall," he says, brushing past her. "You should have gone out on the balcony."

He is still clenching the baguette. He has almost squeezed it into two pieces.

· · ·

Her pillow smells of smoke.

Ellen turns over carefully on the narrow Murphy bed, thinking about the family next door, the strange, heavy girl with the almond-shaped eyes, the skinny mother with her long, red, false fingernails, and the dapper-looking father in plaid shorts, knee socks, and polished loafers.

They had offered her a little glass of eau-de-vie after dinner. It had tasted like fresh raspberries.

He was a translator for some agency dealing with refugees down in Geneva. She asked him about his job. He began to tell her about a hospital where sick children had been hacked to death with a machete, but his wife had grabbed his arm, and his daughter had cried out, "No, Papa, you mustn't talk about it anymore!"

He had closed his eyes, shuddering all over.

"I'd better go," Ellen said, standing up. She felt flushed and exposed. She didn't know what to do.

She had thanked the mother and daughter for dinner. The daughter reached for her cane and followed her back to the open door of her apartment.

"It's cold in here," the daughter said. "But the smoke's gone. I'll close your balcony door."

The burned mess was still in the sink. A breeze was riffling the pages of her manuscript. A few sheets had drifted to the floor. Ellen stooped down and began to pick them up.

The daughter, about to slide the door shut, stepped out on Ellen's balcony instead. She pressed her body against the rail, looking out.

"What is it?" Ellen came up beside her. She could tell the girl wanted to talk to someone. She wished she had caught her name, but she was too embarrassed to ask her for it now.

"Just look," the girl said softly.

The full moon illuminated the still sea of mist below, and Ellen would not have been surprised to see a ship, an old Spanish galleon, emerge from that crag of cloud across the valley, or some dolphins leaping up to play in the moonglow. She fancied that the scene was a reflection from the moon itself, a mirror of the pure lunar landscape.

"How can it be so beautiful?" the girl asked. "What does it mean?"

Ellen stared at her. "What does it mean?" she repeated stupidly.

"I'm sorry about Papa. He reads all these documents, he hears horrors. And they're all true."

"Yes, it's a terrible job," Ellen said. "I never thought about it before."

"He feels so helpless."

"Everyone feels helpless."

"But why?" The girl was gripping the handle of her cane tightly in one fist. "Because look at this—have you ever seen anything so beautiful?"

"No," Ellen said. She felt a tender, scented breeze against her face, a breeze from the moon, perhaps.

"Why are we looking at the moon? Why are we here?"

Ellen looked down at the page she was holding. She saw some words across it. Inexplicably, they made her want to cry. She was a biographer, and her task was to answer this girl's question by reconstructing a life. What did it mean for Katherine Mansfield to live up on this mountain after the war in which her brother had been killed, looking out at this natural beauty, when she could hardly breathe and every day she coughed up another mouthful of her own blood, but still she wrote down words? She didn't know, and she was already done with the book.

"I don't know why we're here," Ellen said. "But I can't help looking at the moon."

The girl drew a deep breath. Suddenly she laughed. "I don't know what we're talking about."

"Me, neither." Ellen smiled at her.

They'd said goodnight, and Ellen pulled down the Murphy bed from the wall.

Now she wonders if she'll sleep tonight. She can still taste the raspberries. The glass shimmered in her hand. The girl's cane was carved ebony, with a gold band around the top. She wore a lot of lipstick, but she wasn't pretty. The mother's red fingernails passing the bread basket had repulsed her. That young man from below had been brandishing a baguette like a phallic symbol. She laughed. The answer to everything these days was supposed to be sex, like children's games where you had to find the picture in the dots. Evan had always fallen asleep with his hand on her thigh. She missed that, the weight of his hand. She'd dreamed about him almost every night. He'd come into the room and stand at the foot of her bed and say nothing, and she'd wake up with a start, realizing that he was a ghost.

.　　.　　.

The mist swirls up from the valley, and the form of a woman takes shape. She's been summoned by a dream, but she's invisible. She's hoping that Rilke has been dreamed back into existence tonight, for she wants to talk. She finds him waiting for her on a red bench.

"They're wondering what life means," she says.

He laughs. He hands her a blue wildflower that he's just plucked. "I heard them talking. I wanted to give them a copy of my poems."

"Do you really think it's enough?"

"Don't you? All your beautiful stories?"

"Yes, at times, but I still get afraid. What are they doing down there? It's worse than ever."

"Oh, my dearest, don't think about it."

She looks at the little flower. She can see it through her transparent hands. It has no scent.

"Look at the moon," he says. He wishes he could put his arm around her, but he knows she'd evaporate under his touch.

She looks up. The cliffs of the moon seem both faraway and very close. She feels a tightness where her chest once was, a fearful throbbing in her absent heart.

The Ugly Virgin

The countryside trembled beneath a thin white vapor, but already the hillside pastures were brightening from a pale chartreuse to a dark, wet green. Rachel watched from the hotel balcony that overlooked the square. All at once, a granite peak swept into view across the river. It was going to be a beautiful day, exactly what she had been dreading.

"Wow," David said softly. "So there are Alps here after all." He came up behind Rachel, put his arm around her, and leaned down to brush his cheek against her forehead. She pressed against him, enjoying his warmth in the chilly air. "So how's the foot?"

"Let me see." Rachel took a few steps, scaring away two sparrows who had been pecking at crumbs. Each time she lifted her heel, a sharp pain twisted across the top of her foot. Three days ago she had stumbled coming down a mountain trail, and a dislodged rock had landed on her boot.

"I'll have to stay off it some more," she said.

David looked down at her foot. "It isn't swollen. That's a good sign." He took a deep breath. "What air! It smells like dew and pine needles. Are you sure you won't mind if Glenna and I hike without you?"

Rachel glanced down the balcony. Glenna's door was shut, though the curtains were half open. The other rooms on this side of the hotel seemed to be empty, for the metal louvered shutters were rolled down tightly. "I said you should go if the weather was good, didn't I?"

"Glenna's really a great person," David said.

"She's very intense."

"But she's not fake. She means everything she says."

"Listen," Rachel said. "What's that?"

"Cowbells." David leaned out over the balcony. "And here they come."

Brown cows were streaming across the bridge and into the square. They had huge, swaying udders and clanking bells around their thick necks. As they came closer, Rachel noticed a few shaggy goats mixed in with the herd, and one sheep with a black face. Three tanned men in blue jeans, who looked like cowboys, strode alongside the herd, calling and cajoling over the noise of the bells. Rachel leaned over the rail with David. He put his arm around her waist. She glanced up at him, thinking how handsome he was, even in the morning when his face was still peppered before his shave. He had blue-black hair, pale skin, and thick, arched eyebrows that gave him a faraway, dreamy look. After the disillusionment of her first marriage, she had not expected to be so happy again.

A soft voice made them jump. "What a wonderful alarm clock."

They hadn't heard Glenna's door open. Now she came toward them, smiling and yawning. She was wearing a long pink T-shirt through which Rachel could see her nipples. She arched her tanned bare feet up and down against the chilly concrete.

Rachel glanced at David. He was smiling back at Glenna. "This place is famous for its cheese."

"Then we'll have to get some famous cheese for lunch." Glenna leaned over the railing beside Rachel. Her short blond hair smelled of lavender shampoo. "I wish I could wake up to cowbells every morning. What a glorious day. Look at the mist—just rolling and tumbling over itself."

Three sheepdogs ran past, barking. The herd disappeared down a street leading out to the countryside.

"There's a steeple," David said, pointing.

"That's the Abbey Church of Notre Dame," Rachel said.

"Oh, it's so beautiful here, isn't it?" Glenna said, her arm brushing Rachel's. "Especially after Chamonix. I bet you can hike here without running into a million people on the trail. Rachel, how's your foot?"

"It's still sore," Rachel said.

"Oh, what a shame." Glenna sighed. "Well, we're not going to abandon you, are we, David? I'd be happy to just sit on the balcony all day."

"No, please," Rachel said, her mouth as dry as it was in the courtroom when she defended a client she knew was guilty. "I want you to go hiking without me. I can finish my book or stroll a little."

"You could go look at the church," David said.

"Oh, sure. Don't worry about me. I'll be fine."

"You're sure, Rachel?" Glenna asked.

"I'll be fine."

She couldn't avoid looking directly into Glenna's eyes, which were wide and blue and full of the same mysterious depths that had attracted her to Glenna ten years ago, when they had both worked as waitresses in Chamonix for no salary except room and board and tips. Ten years ago Glenna had been her best friend, someone to whom Rachel had confided everything. She remembered long, passionate conversations on rainy Sunday mornings. While the two Italian waitresses were at mass, she and Glenna had talked over their lovers, both past and present, with a frankness that amazed Rachel in retrospect. Up in Glenna's narrow little room, with the pine boughs swishing against the mullioned windows, they'd sit facing each other in two armchairs, wrapped in their bath-robes, their feet stretched out and tucked against each other's hips, smoking and talking and drinking cups of chocolate. Rachel, just out of college, liked to analyze her own turbulent emotions, which kept taking her by surprise, while Glenna, three years older and much more experienced, advised her on the true nature of sex, which she considered to be a more in-tense form of communication. Rachel had admired Glenna's ability to separate sensuality from love. She even forgave Glenna—though it had been a troubled month before she could speak to her after their quarrel—when she found out that Glenna had spent a night with the French climber whom Rachel had fallen in love with, whose brooding character and sexual techniques she had previously discussed with Glenna in great detail. "We were having such a deep conversation," Glenna had said, justifying herself, "that we had to have an outlet for our intimacy. We *needed* to sleep with each other. There was no other end to that conversation, don't you see? But it doesn't mean we're in love. He talked about you a lot. He loves you, not me."

Now Rachel realized that she had been able to forgive Glenna because she had chosen to blame the French climber for the betrayal instead of Glenna, and had taught herself to hate him. She took a step back toward David, her stomach shrinking. Six years of practicing family law had convinced her that happiness depended on illusion. Once you knew the truth about someone, it ate at you like a cancer.

"Let's get some breakfast," David said, draping his arm around Rachel's shoulders. "We'll see you downstairs in a few minutes, Glenna. I'll bring the maps."

Back in the room, Rachel crossed to the dresser to find a barrette. Next to David's shaving cream, she saw the snapshot which she had brought from home. It showed Glenna and Rachel standing with their arms around each other in front of l'Auberge de l'Ange-Gardien where they had worked in Chamonix. Glenna's blond hair curled around her shoulders, while Rachel's fell straight and dark to her waist.

"Were you looking at this, David? I thought I put it away."

"What?"

"This photo." She held it up.

"Oh, yeah," David said.

Rachel looked at the photo again. Glenna was a foot taller than Rachel. Her arm was tightly clasped around Rachel's shoulders, while Rachel's hand was just visible at Glenna's waist. After that year of working in France, they had both gone back to America, Glenna home to California, and Rachel to law school in Boston. They had exchanged a few phone calls, then some long letters, then some short letters, and finally just an occasional postcard or friendly note at Christmas. They had both married, and gotten divorces, but Glenna had remained single while Rachel had remarried. In her last note Rachel had mentioned that she and David, her new husband of less than a year, had just bought tickets to Paris, and were planning to drive around Europe that summer. Out of the blue, Glenna had called. What luck! She was going to be in Europe that summer, too, looking around for herbal cosmetics to sell through her mail-order boutique. So why not meet in Chamonix for a few days, and stay as guests at the old Auberge where they had once worked? Rachel had eagerly agreed to the plan.

Never, never go back! She knew that now. L'Auberge de l'Ange-Gardien had been remodeled and enlarged into le Grand Hôtel Ange, and the slopes were covered with new holiday flats and construction cranes. And though Glenna had not changed, and kept trying to draw Rachel into long, confessional chats, Rachel found that she didn't like to talk about her personal life in such frank detail anymore. Her reticence had caused Glenna to begin to look at her speculatively. Rachel often caught her looking at David, too.

They had planned to be together for only a few days, but without consulting Rachel, David had invited Glenna to drive back to Paris with them. Since Chamonix had been so disappointing, they had decided to stop for a couple of days in a mountain town no guidebooks touted, and had picked Abondance in the mountains above Évian. When Rachel sprained her foot, neither David nor Glenna had suggested an alternate plan.

Rachel tucked the snapshot back into the outer pocket of her toiletry bag, and turned around briskly. "You know David, maybe I will go hiking after all. I think my foot's better."

David looked at her. "Don't cripple yourself."

She reached under a chair and pulled out her hiking boots. She took off her sandals, pulled on thick wool socks, and gingerly fitted her right foot into the boot. She laced it loosely. Then she stood up, pretending to comb her chin-length hair, but actually testing her weight for pain.

The restaurant downstairs was bright with sunlight. A big chrome bar shone along one wall. There was a beamed ceiling. Small tables with cane-bottomed chairs were arranged in two rows. Only one was set for breakfast. As Rachel and David pulled out their chairs, they heard Glenna humming something, and in a moment she had joined them. A girl in a red apron came through swinging doors from the kitchen to see what they wanted for breakfast.

"Deux cafés au lait et une tasse de thé avec citron," Rachel said. "That's right, isn't it, Glenna?"

Glenna nodded, tilting her head to listen as Rachel continued to talk to the girl in French. The girl went out.

"What else did she say?"

"She wanted to know if we were staying another night and I said yes. There's going to be dancing on the square tonight."

"Oh, wonderful," Glenna said. "I hope they'll let us join in. I feel like dancing tonight, don't you? Oh, that's right. Your foot."

"Rachel's hiking with us after all," David said.

"Well, good." Glenna looked surprised. She glanced quickly at Rachel, then away.

The girl came back with a tray. She set down a basket of bread, a teapot and a coffeepot. She went over to the bar and began steaming milk.

"I think it's great that you haven't lost your French," Glenna said to Rachel as she dipped her tea bag up and down. "Mine's gone completely. You know, I kept a journal in Chamonix, mostly in English but partly in French. When I opened it this spring, I could barely read the French parts—I didn't even recognize some of the tenses I'd used. Isn't that strange? But your French is as good as ever."

"I spent a lot of summers in Quebec," Rachel said.

"Did you keep a journal that year?" David asked Rachel.

She shook her head.

"Oh, that's too bad," Glenna said. She smiled into Rachel's eyes, and Rachel had to make a great effort not to look away. "It would have been fun to compare notes. I used to write down things you told me. Maybe they're things you've forgotten."

"What things?" Rachel asked.

Glenna glanced briefly at David. "Oh, different things. About your orgasms, for example."

"My orgasms? You wrote down stuff I told you about my orgasms?"

Glenna nodded. "I thought you were writing down things about me, too."

"Well, I wasn't," Rachel said sharply.

David laughed. "You two are funny. I was just looking at that snapshot of both of you again this morning." He was sitting across the table from Rachel and Glenna, and now he reached out both hands and cupped their chins. He tilted their faces toward each other. "You haven't changed except for shorter hair."

"I've changed," Glenna laughed. "Look at my biceps." She pulled away from David and flexed her shapely arm. "And I think Rachel's changed, too," she added. "She's changed very subtly. She's—I don't know, I guess it's just being a lawyer."

"Everybody hates lawyers," Rachel said.

"She certainly doesn't have any muscles." David dropped his hand away from Rachel's chin. "My bird-size wife," he said fondly.

The girl came over with the foaming pitcher of milk. Rachel busied herself with her coffee, trying to hide her anger. Bird-size wife! David had never, never referred to her height like that before.

After breakfast, they bought some bread, two bottles of Evian water, and a hunk of Abondance cheese. Workmen in blue smocks were putting up a tent on the square, and a big sign said "Fête et Bal."

"Looks like we'll have a good view of the dancing," David said. "I hope they wear Alpine costumes."

Glenna stopped for a moment, glancing around. The cafes were empty. A few old men had set out chairs in the sun. "Doesn't look like there'll be much of an audience."

They followed a one-lane paved road out of town to the trailhead for the Col. At first Rachel concentrated on relaxing her foot with each step, and it did not hurt too much. But after they crossed a little stream, lined with orange tiger lilies, the trail began to climb steeply, and she could feel the tendon across the top of her foot swelling up. She had to pause at the turning for each switchback. She could hear David and Glenna laughing and talking somewhere above her. She forced herself to walk faster, trying to pretend that the pain did not exist.

At the next switchback, they were waiting for her on a flat rock. David had spread the map out over his knees, and Glenna was drinking from an Evian bottle.

She handed the bottle to Rachel. "You look hot."

Rachel wiped the sweat off her forehead, and took the bottle. She pushed back some tall cow parsley and sat down on a granite outcropping. She drank deeply. Her foot began to throb. She loosened the laces.

"Does it hurt?" David asked.

"Not much. Where are we?"

"We should be coming to a meadow pretty soon. There are supposed to be some ruined chalets. Then we climb to the lake. We can have lunch, then head up to the Col. That'll be the steepest part. The view should be terrific."

Glenna stood up. "Ready?"

"Just a minute," Rachel said. "I need to catch my breath." She looked down at the valley below. A big cloud had drifted over, casting the village of Abondance into momentary shadow; but the mountains across the valley appeared sharply in focus, the granite peaks tinted purple. "It's so beautiful here."

"It'll be more beautiful at the top. Come on, now," David said, giving her his hand.

Rachel got to her feet. The pain shot up her leg, but she pressed her lips together.

In a few minutes she stopped to lean against a pine tree, blinking back tears. Glenna's voice floated down from somewhere just above her on the trail, gentle, intimate, clear as a bell: "No, go on David. I am interested."

"Well, at first I wanted to save the world," he said. "The Peace Corps seemed like the way to begin. . . ."

David's voice disappeared like a radio signal. Rachel knew the story he was telling by heart. It was the one about how he had spent two years in the Peace Corps in Paraguay, had discovered Guarani folk music, and had returned home to become a musicologist, not an activist.

Now Glenna was saying something. No, that was only a bird. Rachel reached down to pick up a long, straight branch with a gnarled top. She began to move slowly forward, leaning her weight on the branch with each step.

Sweat was pouring down her face. Her eyes kept curling up with pain. She came to a lichen-covered boulder and sat down. Very gently she unlaced her boot.

In a few minutes she heard steps on the trail. "Rachel!" David called.

"I'm down here," she shouted back.

She began to peel the bark off her branch. David and Glenna came hurrying down the trail, loose pebbles flying out from under their boots.

"You should have stayed off it," David said. He was frowning.

"I'm resting for a few minutes," Rachel said. "Why don't we have lunch? I'm sure I'll feel better after I eat."

"It's too soon for lunch. We should eat at the lake."

"But I'm hungry."

"Why don't you go back, Rachel," David said. "Clouds are moving in from the east. If we don't keep moving, we'll be caught in a storm."

"You don't want to permanently damage your foot," Glenna said.

Rachel glanced up at David and Glenna, who were standing side by side. Some hikers were coming up the trail behind them, a red-faced father with a canvas backpack and an alpenstock, a wheezing mother with puffy, blue-veined legs, and two weary-looking teenage girls in blue jeans.

"Bonjour, Monsieur, Mesdames," the father said, plodding onward as David and Glenna stepped aside. The mother and daughters followed him, their sweating faces lowered. It occurred to Rachel that if they thought anything at all, then they must think that David and Glenna, tall and healthy-looking in their damp T-shirts and hiking shorts, were the real couple, and that she was the weak little friend.

"Oh, what's the use," David said, his face flushing. "Let's just forget this hike. I'm sorry, Glenna."

This was Rachel's cue to tell them to go on without her.

She said nothing. David and Glenna looked at each other.

"Oh, I don't mind going back," Glenna said gently. "Doesn't the abbey look inviting down there. I love the onion-shaped steeple."

They all looked down into the valley.

. . .

As Rachel headed toward the rotting wooden staircase where Glenna had already disappeared with the other dozen tourists who were being shown the treasures of the Abbey Church of Notre Dame, David pulled her back by the elbow.

"You're limping. Why the hell didn't you stay off it, Rachel? Why did you insist on coming?"

"I want to see the abbey."

His lips tightened. "You're so stubborn."

"It doesn't hurt so much in sandals," Rachel said, forcing herself to smile brightly at David, the way she smiled at prosecuting attorneys. She took a deep breath, then hurried up the stairs, trying to use her foot normally while David was watching. The pain was constant now. She felt as if someone had her foot in a vice, and was turning the handle tighter and tighter.

Glenna was yawning at the back of the little group of French tourists who were listening to the guide, a teenage boy in blue jeans with a big key ring on his belt. The walls were covered with hanging vestments labeled by century, some green, some white, and some purple. A few of the embroidered ones were protected with plastic coverings.

"Do you know what the colors mean?" Glenna asked, pinching some green satin between her fingers.

Rachel shook her head.

"This cloth is rotting before our eyes," Glenna said. "Oh, I think I'm going to sneeze. It's so moldy in here." She covered her face with both hands, but didn't sneeze after all.

"Look at the prayer books drying on the radiator," David said, coming up behind them.

"They call them missals," Glenna said. "That's the only thing I know. Imagine believing in this stuff."

The guide had moved over to a wooden chest under a dark painting of a woman and a child on a donkey. He unlocked the chest with a huge brass key.

"What's he saying, Rachel?" David asked.

"He's going to show us the treasure."

The boy swung open the door of the chest. He began to point to golden chalices on the shelves, some with smoky-looking jewels around the rims, crosses with little doors in the center, and round orbs connected with chains. The tourists crowded around, exclaiming, elbowing one another.

Glenna stood on her tiptoes to look over everyone's head. "Aren't they afraid someone will steal that stuff? It should be in a museum."

"See that," Rachel said, pointing to an iron box with a slit in the middle that sat on an oak table. "They're collecting donations to preserve the treasure." She reached in her pocket and dropped a few francs through the slit.

Glenna smiled at David. "Not exactly my kind of cause," she said.

"Nor mine." He smiled back. "It's the ozone layer we need to preserve, not this shit."

Rachel flushed. The guide began to lead the group downstairs again, and she held back until David and Glenna had gone before her. Then she limped down, letting the wobbly banister take as much of her weight as she dared to give it.

The guide had unlocked a side door into the church. He waited for her to pass through, then locked it again with one of the big keys on his belt.

The church was cool and dim, and reminded Rachel of all the other churches she had visited that summer. The stained-glass windows were sunless and gloomy when she looked up, following the sweep of the guide's hand. He led the group to a side altar, where an old woman in a shawl was kneeling before a squat wooden statue. He began speaking volubly, waving his arms.

"My God!" David whispered to Rachel and Glenna. "That's the ugliest virgin I've ever seen!"

Glenna smothered a laugh.

The homely, carved virgin wore a satin gown, an embroidered veil, and a jeweled crown. A tiny, stiff-looking child had been stuck on her knee.

"What's he saying?" David asked Rachel.

"He says there used to be a fifteenth-century statue here, Our Lady of Abondance. But a few years ago somebody broke into the church, decapitated a lot of other statues, and Our Lady disappeared. They replaced the famous statue with this one."

"Look at her nose," Glenna said. "Look at her funny eyebrows. She's all out of proportion."

"Mostly head except for that big wooden hand sticking out." David grinned. "Oh, oh, that reminds me of the tip." He reached into his pocket.

The guide had opened a small door that fit inside one of the enormous wooden doors of the church. Everyone filed by, pressing francs into his hand.

Outside, the sky was bright but overcast. The tops of the mountains had disappeared. Two lean, red-cheeked young men in hiking shorts, their shirts stuck to their backs with sweat, passed them, smiling broadly. Their boots were dusty. One of them carried a bottle of wine by the neck.

"Looks like they had a good hike," Glenna said, looking after them regretfully. "I saw them ahead of us on the trail."

"How about a beer?" David asked. "That should cheer you up."

"Right," Glenna said. "I like the looks of the Café des Touristes. It's the one with the awning. I know it's going to rain."

David and Glenna walked briskly ahead, no longer slowing their steps for Rachel. They were already seated by the time she reached the cafe, which was directly across from the tent with rolled-up sides that had been erected on the square for the bal. She pulled out a chair and sank down with relief. A waiter in a wrinkled white shirt took their order and returned with three foaming beers. He set them down on top of cork coasters. Then he returned with three small casseroles of baked cheese, a plate of new potatoes, and some bread.

"So this is the Bertha," David said. "Pretty good."

"Le Berthoud," Rachel said.

A van pulled up, then a truck. Several teenagers began to unload large speakers and a set of drums. "That's funny," David said as the drummer began to warm up on the makeshift stage. "I expected lederhosen and accordions."

Glenna rolled back her shoulders happily. "I hope you aren't down on rock, David. There's nothing I'd rather do tonight than dance. Nothing."

"Me, neither," David said. He looked at Rachel.

She smiled at him. "My foot's much better," she lied. The pain was jolting up her nerves, so that her whole leg was aching. She felt sick to her stomach. "Look," she said, pointing. "Lightning. Over the mountains."

David and Glenna turned to look out. Distant thunder roared.

"It's getting dark," David said.

"Our Lady of Abondance protect us," Glenna said, making a mock cross with her left hand.

"How can they worship such an ugly virgin?" David laughed, finishing his beer. He looked around for the waiter.

"Speaking of virgins, has Rachel ever told you that story?" Glenna asked.

"What story?"

"The story of how she lost her virginity. It's so funny. You mean she's never told you?"

"No," David said. He looked at Rachel.

Rachel looked at Glenna, her hand tightening around her beer glass. "It's not really that funny," she said.

"Oh, it's a great story. Even if I hadn't written it down, I would never have forgotten it. You ought to tell David."

"Oh, go on," David said, reaching over and patting Rachel's knee. "It was a long time ago. We all did crazy, funny things when we were kids."

Rachel shook her head.

Glenna laughed. "Oh, don't be silly about it, Rachel. You told me, after all." She smiled at David. "You see, when Rachel was a freshman she had a date with a big man on campus, one of those really handsome tall guys with curly hair who get elected to everything and belong to the right fraternity and all kinds of clubs, but she was still a virgin, and she didn't dare let him know—she'd led him on to think she was a femme fatale, a woman of the world—so she decided she would have to screw someone else first. But who? That was the trouble. So here's what she did."

Abruptly Glenna stopped. She leaned over and put her arms around Rachel. "She really is embarrassed. I won't tell you, David."

Rachel shuddered at Glenna's touch, but she forced herself to smile. "No, go ahead, Glenna," she muttered, knowing Glenna meant to humiliate her. She gulped her beer. The story was one she had told Glenna in Chamonix. In order to lose her virginity, Rachel had spent a night with the friend of a friend, who'd given her the clap. Of course she'd passed it on to the fraternity boy, who told everyone on campus.

"My lips are sealed," Glenna said. "Sorry, David."

"Oh, I'll get the story out of her later." He laughed. "It's wonderful how you two are still such good friends. I've lost touch with all the people I knew in the Peace Corps."

A gust of wind blew. Big drops of rain began to hit the street, smelling of copper. The speakers had just been plugged in, and a blast of electric guitar startled them all. Then thunder roared again, this time louder and closer.

"It's because we're honest with each other," Glenna said loudly, over the music, reaching back to grab her sweatshirt which was slung over the back of her chair. She slipped it over her head, her breasts lifting visibly against her cotton shirt as she raised her arms. David was looking at her, his lips parted. "We care about each other, don't we, Rachel?"

Rachel nodded. She looked at Glenna, considering what to do. Years ago, she had believed that their exchange of confidences had been equal, but she was wrong. Glenna had always been the heroine of her stories, Rachel the fool. Glenna had drawn her out in the guise of giving advice to a less experienced woman, but all along she had tried to put Rachel down by mocking her emotions, by belittling her lovers, or by sleeping with them in order to hurt Rachel. Her power over Rachel gave her such satisfaction that even this afternoon, though Rachel had so far prevented her from being alone with David, her skin glowed vividly and her eyes glittered. She thought she had won.

The rain began to fall in heavy sheets. Glenna made a little shriek. She pushed her chair back, for the rain was blowing in under the awning. Now she was closer to David.

"I love storms, don't you?"

"Yes," he said.

"I've got to find the toilet," Rachel said, standing up. Her leg almost buckled under her, but she quickly grabbed the back of a chair.

The waiter was sitting hunched at a table by the door, looking across at the tent, tapping his foot and smoking a cigarette. He told Rachel where the toilet was, and she went inside behind the bar. A single light was burning in the hall. She found a door, and slid back an outer latch. But when she pulled open the door, and found the light switch, she saw that she'd made a mistake. She was standing in a narrow, window-less storeroom lined with boxes and cans.

The toilet was further down the hall. She used it, but just as she was wiping herself, she heard a loud crack of lightning. The light went out. She groped for the flush chain in the dark, pulled it, then carefully edged her way back down the hall, navigating with her fingertips. The cafe had been plunged into darkness, but as she came around the bar, a jagged flash of lightning lit up the street outside. As if a director had or-dered a spotlight to fall at that very moment, she saw David and Glenna locked in an embrace. David had his arm around Glenna's back. Her face was against his shoulder, as if she had been frightened by the storm and he was comforting her.

The lurid scene disappeared. Rachel counted to five. Then she kicked a chair so that they would hear her. The next flash of lightning helped her reach the table. David and Glenna were seated as if nothing had happened, as if Rachel had only been dreaming.

"The power's out," David said.

"I know." Rachel sat down. Thunder roared continually. The band had been silenced. In the flashes of lightning, she could see that they were frantically covering their equipment with tarpaulins.

"I hope it comes back soon," Glenna said. "I have to piss, too."

A flash of lightning zigzagged across the sky, illuminating the mountains. Rachel waited for the thunder to come and go, then she leaned in Glenna's direction. "I'll show you where it is. I know my way in the dark now."

"Oh, great," Glenna said. They both stood up. Rachel took her arm. They made their way inside.

"God, it's dark in here," Glenna said.

"It's behind the bar, the first door," Rachel said. "Here, I'll open it for you."

She felt around until she found the latch of the store-room. She opened the door. "In here. The toilet's at the back, paper on the left."

Glenna passed her in the dark. Rachel smelled lavender. Then she shut the door and latched it.

"Rachel!" Glenna's voice sounded faraway and muffled. Two steps away, and all Rachel could hear was low thunder.

"I think the storm's moving off," David said when she joined him. "The band's setting up again."

"Good," Rachel said.

"Where's Glenna?"

"She's not feeling well. It's her period."

"Oh," David said.

The rain had almost stopped now. The thunder was in the distance. Suddenly the electric guitar broke out into "I Love Rock 'n' Roll." The drummer went wild.

"Isn't she taking a long time?" David asked.

"I'll check." Rachel passed the waiter, who paid her no attention. He was looking longingly across the street at the band. When she stood beside the bar and strained her ears over the loud music, she almost thought she could hear Glenna pounding on the door.

She went back to David. "She wants us to go over to the dance. If she's feeling better, she'll join us. If not, then she's going to bed."

"Too bad," David said.

Rachel stood up, gritting her teeth against the pain in her foot. She reached down for David's hands, smiling tenderly, and pulled him to his feet. "Let's dance," she said. "Let's dance until we drop."

My Sister's Novel

About two months after my older sister had been killed in a car accident, my younger sister, Rosemary, called me from Minnesota. Her voice sounded funny.

"I've been going through her things."

"Yes?"

"Did you know she was writing a novel?"

"A novel! Gail?"

"A real novel," Rosemary said. "All typed up."

"That's—that's wonderful!" I felt a stirring of some emotion other than despair for the first time since I had received the numbing news of Gail's death.

"She must have been working on this novel secretly for years," Rosemary said. "She always loved books."

Yes, I remembered Gail's condo—every room had been full of books, from tattered, well-thumbed Jane Austen paperbacks to heavy, thousand-page volumes about Byzantium or the Civil War. But a novel! Even though Gail had had her nose in some book or other since she was a child, she had never said anything about wanting to be a writer. I was struck by how little I really knew about my sister. One of the things that had shocked me when I heard about her death was that her mind was now closed to me.

When she was younger, Gail had dated a lot, much more than Rosemary and I. But she, too, had never married. I wondered why. Twice she had been engaged. She had never talked—at least not to me—about what had happened.

In the last few months before her death, though, she'd been seeing a man named Eric Johnson. I'd met him for the first time at the wake—a tall, curly-haired lawyer with dark circles under his eyes from crying. Gail had been driving back from his place the night she was killed on I-494.

Eric Johnson had hugged me right in front of Gail's coffin. Past his tweed shoulder, I could see my sister's unbearably still, expressionless face, her black hair curled unnaturally and stiffly around her rouged cheeks.

"I loved her," he said in a broken voice. "I wanted you to know that."

My eyes had filled with tears. If Gail had lived, she might have married this man. He might have become my brother-in-law. Had she wanted a baby? I didn't know any more about Gail than the acquaintances who were signing the guest book at the door of the little chapel.

"What should we do with Gail's novel?" I could hear a lump coming into Rosemary's voice. Because she still lived in Minnesota, it was her job to pack up Gail's belongings and dispose of them.

"Have you read it?"

"I just finished it. I'm no judge of writing, but I thought it was really good. Shouldn't we send it somewhere?"

"What do you mean?"

"To get it published."

"Published!" For a moment I imagined stacks of my sister's novel—her name in big bold letters—piled up on a display table at B. Dalton's. Then I shook myself. "She *never* said anything to you about it?"

"Never," Rosemary said. "I'd like you to read it, Lisa. You were the English major. I'll mail you a Xerox—oh, I wish you didn't live so far away!"

"Me, too," I said. "Yes, send it. I'd love to read it. But as far as publishing it goes—I really don't know anything about that stuff."

"Just read it," Rosemary said. "We'll worry about that later." I could hear her taking a deep breath. "You know, after the library comes for all those boxes. . . . It's awful. Her whole life comes down to a couple of closets full of clothes and a few of the things she took when Dad died. They've already advertised to replace her at the Veterans Administration. I just can't bear it."

"Rosemary," I said sharply. "Don't."

"I'm sorry," she said. "But do you know what I mean?"

"Yes, I do. Send me the novel. What's it called, by the way?"

"There's no title," she said. "But it's historical."

.   .   .

A large package finally came. My hands shook as I took the manuscript out of the box. My sister's life was not over. Her mind and her spirit were still here in these five hundred pages. I remembered some of the big books I had read in college, *Middlemarch, Bleak House, Emma.* It had been years since I'd read anything more than the *TV Guide* or one of those best-selling diet books.

I poured myself a glass of wine and sat down on the couch with "Chapter One." At first I was so excited I could hardly read the sentences. I had to keep going back over them to get the sense.

The first chapter was from the point of view of an old painter named Paolo Latini. He lived in Florence and was painting a fresco on the wall of a chapel. The scene was the Annunciation, and the angel was his masterpiece. The chapter was filled with authentic-sounding technical details about painting.

I read on compulsively, but I felt a shrinking sensation in my stomach. I badly wanted the novel to be good, but by a third of the way through, I had to admit to myself that it was tedious. My sister had done a great deal of research on the sack of Rome in 1527. There was a dizzying array of characters besides the old painter—his daughter, Angela, also a painter who ran around disguised as a boy; Brandano, a half-naked, itinerant preacher; Benvenuto Cellini; a villain named Pompeo Carpi who was plotting to destroy Rome; and a handsome hero named Giovanni who, of course, was in love with Angela.

By chapter ten I began having trouble keeping my eyes open. The conspiracy had gotten so complicated that I didn't know what was going on. Apparently someone named the Constable of Bourbon was marching on Rome, but I wasn't sure why. No one in Rome believed the threat, except the old painter and his daughter, who excitedly tried to warn everyone else, but without success. Meanwhile there was a party at somebody's villa.

When I reached chapter fifteen, I closed my eyes in disappointment. Where was my sister in all these words? The novel was lifeless. Even the character of Angela, who I kept trying to identify with my sister, painted her canvases and performed her heroic deeds in such a dull fashion that my eyes kept skimming ahead, not to find out what was going to happen, but only to get the thing over with.

Two days later, I finally finished the novel. I put it on the top shelf of my closet. But, in bed at night, I kept thinking about it. Was it as bad as I thought? Was there something wrong with me as a reader?

.   .   .

A week or so later I got a call from Rosemary. She sounded excited.

"Have you read it?"

"Yes."

"Well? Isn't it wonderful?"

I took a deep breath. "It's really ambitious."

"Didn't you think the old painter was modeled on Dad? I think you're supposed to be Barbara—Giovanni's sister. And the old peasant woman—the good-hearted one—is Mom, isn't she?"

"Now that you mention it," I said, trying to keep a doubtful tone out of my voice. I couldn't remember any old peasant woman. She must have appeared in the part where I started skimming.

"My favorite part is when Giovanni discovers that his friend, Angelo, is really a girl."

"Yes, that was nice."

"And that scene where Giovanni goes to the Council of Rome, and pleads with the rich men to pay for the defense of the city. What a speech!"

"Yes, it was." *That* part I remembered. The speech—full of windy rhetoric and pompous arguments—had gone on for seven pages without a break.

"Well, I've found a publisher," Rosemary said.

"You have?"

"They'll print 500 copies for $2500."

"You mean we *pay* to have it published?"

"Why not?" Rosemary said. "We could split the cost. It would be a sort of a monument—a remembrance—for her. I saw some samples. They do cloth covers with gilt lettering."

"I don't know, Rosemary," I said. "Are you sure it's—finished? Maybe Gail meant to work on it some more."

"I think it's finished. I think it could be a best-seller. Mr. Venerson, the editor I talked to, says they always send out review copies. If someone in New York liked Gail's book, then it might be reprinted."

I didn't know what to say. Rosemary and Gail, because they had lived so close, had seen each other almost every week. They had been there to comfort our father when our mother died suddenly, and had later cared for our father during those long months when he was in and out of the hospital. I had lived in Chicago for the last twelve years, and had been back only occasionally for visits—and for funerals. I didn't want to hurt Rosemary. I could see that if I told her the truth about the novel, it would be a terrible blow.

"Lisa? Are you still there?"

"I'm here," I said.

"Could you come up this weekend? I've got an appointment set up with Mr. Venerson, and I'd like you to be there."

"Has this—has this editor read the novel?"

"Oh, yes. He really likes it, too. He says a lot of the stuff they publish is just for vanity, but he thinks Gail's novel is the real thing."

"I see. OK, then. I'll take Friday off and fly up. I'll call you back as soon as I know which flight."

I hung up, then called my travel agent to make reservations. Afterwards I wandered around my apartment looking at the framed posters and prints I had brought back from my trips to Europe. Should I have told Rosemary the truth— that Gail's novel was bad, embarrassingly bad? But who was I to say, anyway? In college I had written a few stories, but I had been frank with myself. They hadn't been very good. I had written them only to explore my own personality, and once I had understood myself fairly well, there had been no reason to continue. I was no Virginia Woolf. Now I wrote nothing but letters and interminable memos at the ad agency where I was traffic manager.

I pulled Gail's novel off the shelf. What if I was wrong? I turned to chapter nine and started reading at random: "Angela, still dressed as a boy, searched for Cellini in the lively streets of the artists' quarter across the Tiber. She got directions to his workshop, which was large and spacious and filled with young goldsmiths working on beautiful urns and medals under the direction of Cellini, a broad-shouldered, bearded man with sharp, blazing black eyes. She showed Cellini her paintings and designs and drawings, and he was so impressed he invited her to supper. At supper, everyone got drunk. Cellini pulled a sword on one of his friends, and had to be stopped and mollified by others. He quarreled with his mistress, and kicked her out."

I sighed. No, I wasn't wrong. The whole novel was like reading the summary of some other novel.

. . .

Rosemary met me at the gate. She had a topaz brooch, which had belonged to our mother, on the collar of her coat. There were salt stains on her high, leather boots.

"I'm glad you're wearing a parka," she said, hugging me. "It's really cold. Ten below and dropping."

Outside in the parking lot, the air was like iron. I could feel my nose hairs stiffening.

There were plumes of exhaust pouring out the tailpipes of the cars backed up on the freeway entrance. It took a long time for the heater to warm the car enough for me to take off my gloves.

"I'll get off here," Rosemary said. "We'll drive past the old house. Every now and then I like to drive by."

The residential streets were ploughed but covered with squeaking, packed-down snow. Rosemary drove slowly around the park. This was the neighborhood where we had all grown up. I looked out toward the lake as we passed. The new arc lights by the skating rink made the snow look pinkish.

We turned onto our old street.

"Who lives in the house now?" I asked.

"It was sold again," Rosemary said. "The new people seem to have children."

Tiny, blinking lights had been strung through the branches of the two fir trees in the front yard. The curtains at the picture window were still open to display the lighted Christmas tree. A wreath hung on the front door.

"It looks like we still live there, doesn't it?" Rosemary said in a soft voice. "As if we could walk through the door and there they'd all be, Mom and Dad and Gail."

I had to wipe my eyes with my sleeve. "Let's go," I said thickly. "This wasn't such a good idea."

Rosemary clenched her eyes together tightly. "But we've got something left. We've got Gail's novel. You know, the more I think about it, the more I realize that it's about our family."

I didn't say anything. Rosemary braced herself, and swallowed her tears. "We'll stop at Gail's condo. It's on the way. There are a few things you might want to take."

I almost spoke up to say, *No, let's wait until tomorrow,* but I bit my tongue in time. Rosemary had had to face her loss every day. I had been lucky to live in another town where there were no associations to increase my grief.

Gail hadn't lived far from my parents. We pulled up outside her garage. There were Christmas trees glittering in the windows of most of the other units.

"I've got someone lined up to buy her place," Rosemary said.

She unlocked the front door and we went inside. It was cold. Rosemary switched on the lights.

I looked around at all the cardboard boxes. Many were sealed up, but others still had their flaps open. Boxes were piled on Gail's sofa. Her butcher-block table in the dining area was covered with crystal.

Rosemary picked up a Waterford champagne glass and held it up to the light. "I was over here last New Year's," she said. "We drank two bottles of champagne. We even talked about taking a trip to Europe together. And she especially wanted to go to Italy—wait, it's coming back to me—she said she'd always wanted to see Venice and Florence. Of course! That was before she met Eric."

"Did Eric know about Gail's novel?"

Rosemary frowned. She set the glass back down on the table. The table shook, and the crystal shimmered and twinkled.

"You know, I never asked him. We got together a few times during those first couple of weeks after the funeral, but I haven't seen him now for about a month. I've been working a lot of overtime."

She sighed. "How about a glass of liebfraumilch? There's a bottle in the icebox."

"Sure."

Rosemary went into the kitchen and came back with a brown bottle. She filled two champagne glasses. "You know, I'd like to see more of Eric—he's such a nice guy. He'll always have Gail in his memory, so that makes him almost a brother, doesn't it?"

"She might have confided in him," I said. "Don't you think she would have told *someone* she was writing a novel?"

"You'd think so. But she never told me."

"She didn't keep a diary, did she?"

Rosemary shook her head. "No. That was one of the first things I looked for." She took off her wool hat. Her hair was glossy black. Unlike me, she had started to rinse out the early grey.

I finished my wine, and Rosemary poured me another glass.

"What about notes for the novel, or a first draft?" I asked.

"I only found what I sent you—there, in that desk."

I looked at Gail's desk. It was a spindly, French Provincial imitation. I remembered that years ago, when I had come up for a short visit in the summer, Gail sat down at that desk to write someone a note on lilac-bordered paper.

"Where's her typewriter?"

"She didn't have one. She must have typed the novel at work." Rosemary suddenly flushed. "What's the matter with you? You don't seem very enthusiastic about publishing Gail's novel."

"Maybe that's not what she wanted," I said lamely.

"Look around you. Look!" Rosemary reached into one of the cardboard boxes and began pulling out objects and setting them on the floor at my feet: a pair of embroidered bedroom slippers, a ceramic piggy bank, a pearl necklace, a leather address book, a jar of purple bath crystals, mittens, a beige slip. She balled the slip in her hand and flung it at me. I caught the cold, slippery nylon against my chest.

"This is all there is left of Gail—just stuff she touched or wore or liked. But this novel—" Rosemary ran over to the little desk and opened the middle drawer. "Here it is! This is her mind, Lisa. This is her soul. She was expressing herself."

She turned away to hide her face. She was about to put the manuscript back in the desk when suddenly she swung back again, holding it against her chest.

"Let's go over and see Eric. I think he should see the novel, too. He loved Gail. And maybe—like you said—she might have talked about it. I guess I'd like to know what she thought about it. How important it was to her."

"Call him, then."

While Rosemary was on the phone, I poured myself another glass of wine and wandered down the hall to Gail's bedroom. The mattress was bare, and the closets were both empty. Even the curtains had been taken down. There were three empty bookcases against the walls. A pair of brass bookends in the shape of owls stood on top of one bookcase, pressed against each other instead of against the row of books they once kept upright. I shivered and turned off the light.

.   .   .

Eric Johnson had a house in a small town beyond I-495. It took us forty-five minutes on the freeway, and then we were out in the country, driving on a sanded two-lane past occasional farmhouses. I was feeling pleasantly drunk. I liked looking at the Christmas lights in the windows across snowy fields.

Rosemary turned into a new development. She seemed to know her way, though the streets had no signs.

"Eric's wife left him right after they built this house," Rosemary said. "That was two years ago."

"I didn't know he'd been married before."

"He told me a lot of things about himself." She sighed. "He really loved Gail. I think they would have gotten married. We might have been bridesmaids."

Rosemary parked behind a Toyota pickup in the well-lit driveway. "I like to think that Gail was very happy when she—passed away. Happier than she'd ever been. She was in love. She'd written a novel. Her life *meant* something."

"She sounded happy the last time I talked to her," I said. "She'd gotten a raise."

"Now we'll have her book to give to people she cared for—Eric, Aunt Susan, her friends at work."

All night I'd been searching for the right words in which to tell Rosemary that Gail's novel wasn't good enough to be published. Now I saw that it was not going to be possible. I was going to have to keep on pretending. I would have to keep my mouth shut, especially tomorrow morning when Rosemary talked to Mr. Venerson, the so-called editor, who surely knew the truth and was just leading her on. I had just the faintest hope that Gail had shown her novel to Eric, and that he, too, thought it was terrible. If he were the one to tell Rosemary, it might not be as painful.

I took Rosemary's arm as we climbed the icy steps to the front door of the trilevel house. Eric must have been looking out for us, for the door opened before we could knock.

"Come in, come in," he said. His face was flushed, and his breath smelled as if he, too, had had a couple of drinks.

He was wearing a thick, dark blue sweater that matched his eyes. "Let me take your coats."

The living room had a cathedral ceiling and a fieldstone fireplace. The carpeting was thick and white. Rosemary immediately pulled off her boots and stepped forward in her stocking feet. The novel was under her arm, wrapped up in a grocery bag. I wiped my shoes on the mat, and checked the soles to make sure they were clean.

"Could I get you a drink? Whiskey? Wine? Or a little Christmas cheer—I've got some eggnog."

"Eggnog sounds fine," I said.

"I'd like a glass of white wine," Rosemary said, and when Eric left the room, she sank back against the cushions of the long, white, sectional sofa. I sat gingerly on the edge of a matching chair, and looked around. Many expensive books of art reproductions were piled up on the glass and chrome coffee table. I read the spines: Botticelli, Fra Filippo Lippi, Cezanne, Vermeer.

Eric came back with two glasses of wine and a cup of foamy eggnog for me. "Freshly made," he said.

"How have you been, Eric?" Rosemary said in a warm, sympathetic voice. "Are you bearing up?"

"I'm taking things a day at a time," he said. "Just a day at a time."

"That's the only way to get through," Rosemary said.

"I've got something to show you, Rosemary. I just found these in a drawer when I was cleaning up the other day." He went over and opened a drawer in one of the end tables. He took out a package of photographs. He handed half the stack to Rosemary, and the other half to me. Then he brought me another glass of eggnog, and refilled Rosemary's glass.

I went through my stack, puzzled. The photos were all of Eric, sitting on a picnic-table bench or standing under a tree. A few were of rocks. One showed an expanse of blurry water.

Finally I came to a photograph of Gail. She was wearing white shorts and a halter top. Her black hair was blowing into her face.

"Gail took most of them," Eric said. "That was our picnic back in July at Minnehaha Falls."

"She looks so happy," Rosemary said, exchanging stacks with me. Her stack included a few more photographs of Gail—Gail pointing at the falls, which were nearly dry; Gail making a funny face; Gail waving a can of beer from the top of a boulder.

"I could make you a set of these," Eric said.

"Oh, please," Rosemary said.

"You really had a good tan last summer," I said, handing my photographs back to Eric.

He laughed. "Thanks to the tanning booth. I had to work just about every sunny weekend—the cases were really piling up. Two or three times I had to cancel on Gail, too." He shook his head sadly.

Rosemary was still looking at the photographs. I finished my second eggnog, which was heavily laced with rum. I needed to use the toilet.

"Uh, could you tell me where the bathroom is?" I asked Eric.

"Sure," he said, standing up. "Just down the hall, third door on the right." He picked up my glass. "How about switching to Scotch? I'm all out of nog."

"Fine," I said. "But just a tad of water."

I felt a little woozy, but I found the bathroom without any trouble and switched on the light. While I was sitting on the toilet I noticed some sheer panty hose drying over the shower curtain.

I flushed the toilet, puzzled. Were they Gail's? Surely not after all this time.

I looked at the tub carefully. There were two bottles of shampoo on the plastic rack, and a bottle of cream rinse. I picked up the bottle of cream rinse. Several long, blond hairs were stuck to the cap.

I stepped out of the bathroom. I could hear Eric and Rosemary talking out in the living room. I knew I wasn't visible in the hallway. I tiptoed down to the end bedroom, which I figured was the master bedroom, and switched on the light.

The king-size bed was unmade and rumpled. An eggnog glass, half-full, was sitting on each nightstand, as if two people had been sitting up in bed after sex, having a drink together. Rosemary's phone call must have interrupted Eric and his new girlfriend.

I caught a glimpse of myself in the mirror over the bureau. I pushed my graying black hair out of my face. I looked like the ghost of Gail. I had all her features, the same shock of hair, but though I was a year younger, I looked pale and washed out. In those few photographs from last summer, Gail had looked firm and healthy, and—I could not deny it, Rosemary was right—she had looked happy.

For a moment, I thought I was looking at Gail, not myself. Her face was sad and distant as if she understood that she had been forgotten. She put her hand to her brow. Then I stepped away, and the mirror was blank again, reflecting only the wall.

I felt a sudden rush of anger against Eric Johnson as I walked down the hall to the living room. It wasn't that he had forgotten Gail in only two months—that was human nature—but it bothered me that he was pretending that he hadn't. I hated his hypocrisy.

Rosemary was smiling. "Eric's been telling me some more things about Gail," she said. "Eric and Gail had signed up to take cross-country ski lessons this winter."

"Oh, really," I said. I picked up my Scotch and took a long drink so I would not have to look at Eric's overly animated face.

"She was determined to learn," he said. "She had a lot of spunk."

Rosemary gave me a little, meaningful smile. "Well, the reason we came over," she said, sitting forward on the sofa and pulling the novel out of the grocery bag, "is that we want to ask you about the novel Gail was writing. We found it in her desk."

A look of surprise, then chagrin, crossed Eric's face. He licked his lips nervously. "Oh, you found it," he said.

Rosemary leaned forward eagerly. "So you know about it."

"Well," he said, clearing his throat and flushing. "You see, it's my novel."

"Yours!" Rosemary looked blank. "What do you mean?"

"I'm a writer," he said. "Or a would-be writer. I haven't ever published anything, but I've been writing to some agents, you see. I've told them about my novel and a couple are interested."

"But why did Gail have it?" I asked hurriedly, for Rosemary had fallen back against the sofa. She looked almost sick. Her glass of wine was trembling in her hand.

"She was kindly going to critique it for me," Eric said. "For grammar."

"Oh, I see," I said. I was watching Rosemary. She had brought her free hand up against her face. I could see that the news was a real shock for her, and I hoped she would be all right. As for me, I felt great relief. My sister had not been responsible for that boring piece of trash. Thank God!

Eric leaned toward me. "Did you read it?"

"We thought it was Gail's."

"I'm sorry," he said. "After the tragedy, I just forgot all about it—that I'd given Gail a copy, I mean. There were so many other things to think about. And later on I just didn't want to bother you, Rosemary, by asking about it—I mean, I've got it on disk. I don't need that copy."

"There wasn't a name on it," I said.

"I didn't give Gail a title page because I'm still not sure of a title. She was going to give me some ideas—I guess she never had a chance to read it." He sighed. "She'd only had it about two weeks." He looked at me closely. "You said you read it?"

"We both read it."

He swallowed, looked down at his glass, then directly at me. "Could I ask you—would you be offended—what did you think of it?"

"I guess we both thought Gail wrote it," I said evasively as I finished my Scotch. "She always liked books."

"But what was your *literary* opinion?"

"Well, I thought—"

"It's wonderful, Eric," Rosemary said breathlessly, wiping her eyes and sitting forward again. The novel slid off her lap. "I'm sure Gail would have loved it."

"Let me get you some more wine," Eric said eagerly. He leapt up and came back from the kitchen with the bottle. As he passed me this time, I noticed a blond hair stuck to the rough wool of his sleeve.

He sat down across from Rosemary. His eyes glowed as he waited for more praise. "What did you think of my characters? Did they seem real to you?"

"I think your novel needs a lot of work, Eric," I said.

"Don't listen to Lisa," Rosemary said, laughing a little. "She's always very critical."

"If you want an honest opinion, Eric, I thought it was pretty boring," I said.

"My opinion is honest, too," Rosemary said. She was glaring at me, trying to shut me up. "I was moved by your novel, Eric. It's one of the best novels I've ever read."

I couldn't stop myself now. I never could when I drank too much. "It's a terrible novel," I said. "It's embarrassing." I stood up, looking directly at Rosemary. "I'm delighted to find out that Gail didn't write that piece of nonsense."

Eric looked devastated.

"But you said you liked it!" Rosemary cried, her voice trembling. "You said it was ambitious. You mean you only liked it because you thought Gail wrote it?"

"I just didn't want to hurt your feelings," I said. The furniture in the room was beginning to waver and float. Rosemary and Eric seemed brightly lit and two-dimensional, as if they were really only paper dolls.

"You always thought you knew more than the rest of us," Rosemary said bitterly. "Anyway, you're drunk."

"You're not exactly sober," I said. "Neither was Gail the night she was killed."

Rosemary swallowed. She stood up. "You think you're better than everyone."

"At least I'm not a hypocrite," I said. I glanced at Eric. I think I was about to tell Rosemary about his new girlfriend, but the expression on his face stopped me. He looked as if someone had just punched him.

"Let's go, Lisa," Rosemary said. "I'm going to take her home, Eric. I'm sorry about this. She doesn't know what she's saying."

Rosemary had my parka. She thrust it at me angrily, and somehow I got my arms in the sleeves. Then we were out the door. The cold hit me like a black wave.

I heard Rosemary saying good-bye to Eric, and I started down the stairs. I felt my feet slide out from under me on the ice, and a second later I was lying on my back at the bottom of the stairs. I couldn't move. I felt as if I were one of those trick flies frozen into an ice cube. I looked up through the cold at the stars. I saw what Gail had seen in that second when she lost control, and even though Rosemary was screaming and pulling me to my feet only a few seconds later, and I knew that I was unhurt except for a bruised shin, my shadowy life had already passed before my eyes.

Do Not Forsake Me, Oh My Darling

At six o'clock one March evening in Dixon, Nebraska, four customers, at different tables, were eating an early dinner in the Starlight Bar and Grill when a tall man in a cowboy hat came rustling through the bead curtain which separated the entrance hall from the dining room. The man's hat was covered with snow and resembled an absurd wedding cake.

"Good God!" exclaimed a dental supply salesman, who was on his way back to Kansas City. "When did that start?"

"Half hour ago. It's a blizzard." The man took off his cowboy hat and dumped it upside down. Snow slid off the brim and made a mound at his feet before beginning to melt into the dirty green carpet.

Two regulars, an old woman in a green polyester pants suit, and a retired farmer, who were already eating slabs of lemon meringue pie, pushed back their plates in alarm.

An attractive middle-aged woman, her black hair speckled with grey, who had been reading a thick paperback while she picked pale tomato wedges out of her salad, gave a little shudder. She was a flutist, and was on her way to the Rosebud Indian Reservation in South

Dakota, where she was going to give a recital and teach a demonstration class for children.

"Is it real bad?" asked the old woman.

"I had to leave my jeep down at the 7-Eleven and feel my way along the walls. You can't see an inch in front of your face." The man placed his cowboy hat carefully on a paper place mat. He brushed more snow off the shoulders of his rawhide jacket and sat down opposite his hat.

The flutist, who wore an elegant black blouse, tight jeans, and Italian shoes, looked at him more closely. He had tousled, dull-colored hair—blond hair that was turning grey. His eyes were sharply blue in his lined face. Her heart began to beat very fast. Did she recognize him? No, no, it couldn't be.

The waitress came in with a tray. A long strand of grey hair had fallen across her forehead, and she shook her head a couple of times to get it out of her eyes. "Look what you've done to my floor, Nick," she laughed. "What'll it be? Bourbon and water?"

"And the menu. Looks like I'll be having supper here tonight, Mary."

"You mean it's blowing that hard?"

"I've never seen it blow this hard, not in seventeen years."

The phone rang from the bar. Mary put the tray down on an empty table, and hurried to answer it. The man named Nick turned to grab a bottle of catsup from another table, and the flutist quickly averted her face. It's him, she thought. It's really, really him!

And although she had barely thought of Nick Goddard in the last twenty years, for she had had many lovers and two husbands, she remembered in a dizzy rush that she had loved him once, desperately. She had met him on a student train as it pulled out of Athens, headed up through Yugoslavia for Amsterdam. For three days in the crowded, second-class, couchette compartment, they had been able to do nothing more than talk about themselves and hold hands and press against each other and kiss furtively. Her desire for him had reached such a crescendo that once, when she stood up to go to the toilet, her legs had trembled so much that she had grabbed the luggage rack to keep from falling. She had staggered down the corridor, which was crowded with sweating, babbling Yugoslavian peasants with their baskets and babies and chickens, light-headed and happier than she had ever been in her life. Now, as if a genie had been released from a bottle, an ancient emotion flooded her, and she felt exactly as she had felt all those years ago. But how was that possible?

The old farmer, who wore overalls and a plaid flannel shirt, got up and went out through the bead curtain. He came back in a moment, rubbing his face, a few snowflakes in his hair.

"Looks bad," he reported. "Fifty-mile-an-hour winds, I'd say."

Mary, the waitress, returned from the phone. "That was the sheriff's office," she announced to the room at large. "They want everyone who's here to stay here until it lets up."

"I've got to get back to the motel," the salesman said, pushing back his chair.

"Just relax and eat," Mary said, bringing him one of the plates from the tray. "Here's your T-bone."

"Mary, my daughter's expecting me!" The woman in the green pants suit began to wring her hands together nervously. "I'm baby-sitting tonight."

"Better telephone her, hon."

"You're staying at the motel, too, aren't you?" the salesman called over to the flutist.

"Yes," she said, startled to hear herself addressed. "I drove over. I'm parked around the corner."

"The tow trucks can't even leave the garage," Mary added, placing a plate of fried chicken in front of the flutist.

"But I listened to the forecast," the salesman said. "It wasn't supposed to snow!"

"Going to lose some cows tonight, Nick?" the old farmer asked.

"Hope not," Nick said.

A fat man in a white apron suddenly appeared from the kitchen. He was wiping his hands on a towel. "We're in for it, folks. Radio says they don't expect any letup until tomorrow morning."

The flutist took a bite of her chicken. She looked secretly at Nick's profile as the waitress served him his bourbon and water, and handed him a menu. So he didn't recognize her. Twenty years was a long time. But how had he come to be here, in the middle of Nebraska, dressed like a cowboy? She had a sudden flash of his white, naked, nineteen-year-old body pressed against her in a sagging bed in the little canal-house pension in Amsterdam where they had gone as soon as the train arrived. Although they were both covered with three-days accumulation of sweat and grime, they had ignored the shower down the hall and had made love over and over again until they were so exhausted they fell asleep in each other's arms. She could still remember the shape of his buttocks under her hands.

She looked at him again. His lips seemed bitten and harder. The skin was sagging a little under his jawline. He was heavier, too. He had talked about being an actor, then. He had been funny and witty, always pretending to be someone else. What was he doing here in Nebraska of all places?

Of course she had changed, too. Back then her black hair fell to her waist. She wore sundresses with cutout backs or hot pants with white stockings. She remembered a pair of tan shoes with high wedges that made her taller, brought her almost to his shoulder. That was the summer she had decided to give up the flute. She had gone for four months without practicing.

"Well, you know, folks," the waitress was saying as she came around with the coffeepot, "you've got yourself stranded in the right restaurant tonight. At the Pizza Palace you'd have to sleep on the floor, but this place used to be a hotel restaurant. The hotel closed down about five years ago, but some of those rooms above us still got beds in them, and I bet we could rustle up some sheets and blankets."

"I've got paperwork to do," the salesman complained. "And it's all back at the motel." He got up from his table. "I'm going to take a look. I've driven in storms before."

"Not this one," Nick said. He took a long swig of bourbon.

The salesman left the room. He came back shortly, shaking his head. "It's a whiteout, a real whiteout."

The flutist finished her chicken. "Any dessert, hon?" the waitress asked.

"I'd like a brandy."

"Sure thing." The waitress approached Nick. "Ready to order?"

"What's the special?"

"Chicken-fried steak."

"I'll take the special. And another one of these." He pointed to his empty glass.

The waitress came back to the flutist's table. "My mind's not what it used to be, hon. Can't remember my own name, some days. What did you just order?"

"Brandy," the flutist repeated. Nick had turned around while he talked to the waitress. Now he was staring hard at the flutist, squinting a little. After the waitress left, he got up and came over to her table.

"I think I used to know you. Aren't you Susan?"

"Yes," she said, flushing.

"I'm Nick."

"Nick," she repeated. "Of course. Will you join me?"

He sat down, looking at her intently. "Funny to run into you here."

"I just gave a recital over at the junior college in Norfolk. I'm on my way to South Dakota. That is," she laughed nervously, "if the storm lets up."

"So you still play the—violin, was it?"

"Flute."

He nodded. "Good for you."

"Do you live around here, then?"

"I have a few acres and some cows about ten miles from here."

"How did you become a rancher?"

"I'm not exactly a rancher. My wife teaches history at the high school over in Norfolk. I work for the PBS station over there."

"Acting?"

"I do a local news show."

"But how strange that you're in Nebraska!"

He shrugged. "It's not so strange. I grew up around here, though I guess when I went off to Boston for college I never expected to be back. But here I am. Marnie—my wife—was born in Dixon." He glanced quickly at her bare, ringless hands. "You're not married."

"Not now," she said. "I was."

"So you travel around playing the flute. That must be interesting."

"I have a very minor concert career. Mostly I teach."

The waitress returned with the drinks. She seemed surprised to see that Nick had switched tables. "Special will be out in a sec, Nick."

"Thanks, Mary."

"You two know each other?"

"We're old friends," Nick said.

Mary nodded. She set the glasses on paper coasters, then picked up her tray and disappeared into the kitchen.

"I guess you know everyone around here, then," Susan said.

"You bet. We all mind each other's business."

They fell silent. Susan looked at Nick out of the corner of her eye. He was thinking, frowning a little in a way that was familiar to her. She remembered how he had sat frowning that way on their last night together in London. Then he had told her that he didn't want to see her back in the States—it couldn't work, he said, they were going to school in different parts of the country, and he didn't believe in long-distance romances. He wanted to make a clean break now. He wanted to say good-bye forever.

She had protested, she had wept, but over and over, in a tender voice that filled her with horror because the words were so cruel, he had insisted. He had been hurt before, and he couldn't bear to be hurt again, he said. She accused him of having another girlfriend back home, but he vowed that that wasn't it. He knew she wouldn't continue to love him, that it was just a summer romance, and he wanted it to stop now, not later.

On the plane, all the way back to New York, she had hidden her face in a pillow. She had been numb and miserable her first month back in college. Then she had rededicated herself to the flute. In December she met Julian, the pianist she had eventually married. And in January, when Nick called her at last and told her that letting her go had been the mistake of his life, that he could not forget her no matter how he tried, she had been cold and distant. She was involved with someone else, she told him with calm satisfaction. And after she hung up, she rarely thought of him again, and only in connection with certain European cities.

But now she was shocked to find old emotion still so strong and untouched inside her. She looked at Nick.

The lights flickered. "Whoops!" Mary cried. She placed Nick's plate expertly in front of him with one quick hand. "You better call that daughter of yours right away, Emmy. Phone lines might go down."

"Oh, dear, oh, dear." The old woman got up and hurried around past the bar.

The lights went out completely. Susan gasped, but then the lights came back on again. She and Nick were staring into each other's eyes.

She smiled at him. "Remember the tunnels?"

He nodded. She thought he looked uneasy. Whenever the train had entered a tunnel, she and Nick had kissed passionately, ignoring the other students in their compartment. The memory of his hand inside her shirt was shockingly vivid.

"We're bound to lose the lights sooner or later," Mary said cheerfully, wiping her hands on her white uniform. "Nick, when you're finished, would you go upstairs and check out some of them rooms—see which ones are in good enough shape to put people in? I'll look for those old linens. Once the lights go, it'll be dark as a dungeon in here. Hope I can find a flashlight."

Nick ate rapidly, washing his steak and fries down with the bourbon. Susan sipped her brandy. She felt as if a window had opened up inside her brain. She remembered things she thought she had forgotten forever. She saw the hotel room in Paris with the brass bedstead, and the little rickety table with claw feet where the concierge placed the breakfast tray each morning. She could taste the scalding chocolate.

The lights flickered again. Nick pushed his plate back and stood up.

"Can I come up with you?" Susan asked.

"Sure," he said.

Susan grabbed her purse. She followed him around to the other side of the bar, and out through a dirty glass door. They were in a dim hall, lit only by the light coming through from the dining room. Now they could hear the wind howling.

Nick fumbled for switches. Lights flashed on. A small, crooked chandelier glittered over a dusty hotel desk littered with junk, an accumulation of old lamps, vases, file boxes and tangled extension cords.

Susan followed Nick up some uncarpeted stairs. At the landing, she looked up and saw a pair of steer horns hanging on the wall. One of the tips was broken.

Nick looked back over his shoulder. "You know, before they built the motel, this was the only place in town you could stay."

They stood at the head of the stairs, looking down a long corridor. The carpeting had been torn out, but there were still tacks here and there in the stained oak floor.

"I know they've sold some of the beds and dressers, but I guess there should be a few rooms that are passable. You take that side of the hall."

"Okay," Susan said, opening the first door on her right. She reached around and found the light switch. The room was full of cardboard cartons and nothing else. The wind was rattling the window.

She went back out into the hall and tried the next room. Here there was a bed with a stained mattress. She put her hand on the wooden bedpost. The frame wobbled unsteadily.

The next room was eerily lit from the window, as if a streetlight were just outside. Without turning on the light, she could tell that the room held only two battered dressers, the matching mirrors propped against the wall. But she walked inside anyway and went to look out the window. She could feel the cold wind coming through the cracks.

At first she could see nothing outside but a strange, shifting white light. But if she kept her attention riveted, and tried not to blink, there were occasional miraculous sweeps of vision as the wind shifted and the violently falling snow was momentarily directed backwards. Once she saw the whole globe of the streetlight itself, which was only a few feet from the window. Once she caught a view of the drugstore across the street, snow drifted up against its plate-glass window. And once she saw the white mounds of cars down in the street below. Then the wind blew fiercely again, and she could see nothing but the driving whiteness of the flakes.

When she turned on the light in the next room, she saw that it was usable. A sturdy bed stood between the two windows. There was even an old Gideon Bible on the nightstand. The mirror was still hanging over the dresser.

"How you doing?" she heard Nick call from across the hall.

"This room's fine," she called back.

"I found a couple, too. Let's try the third floor."

Just then the lights went out. Susan gasped. The room she was in was very dark. This time the lights stayed out.

"You okay?"

"I can't see."

"I'll be there in a minute. My eyes are adjusting."

She heard his step in the corridor. "In here," she called.

He stumbled once, then she saw a darker bulk in the darkness. She moved toward it.

Their arms brushed. "Hope Mary's found a flashlight," Nick said. Susan thought he sounded embarrassed.

"Maybe the lights will come back on."

"I doubt it." He had moved over to a window. Her eyes had adjusted, and she could see his silhouette against the pale square. She moved over beside him. The door in her mind was opening wider and wider. She was inside it now. The colors were bright and vivid. She was nineteen. She wanted him to come inside with her. She could hear him breathing as she brushed against him.

"Some storm," he said. He swallowed hard.

"Nick," she said softly, "do you remember that little tune you used to hum all the time when we were together?"

He shook his head. "I used to hum a lot of things."

She hummed the tune, then whispered softly, "'Do not forsake me, oh my darling.'"

"Did I hum that?"

"All the time."

"I've forgotten."

"You haven't forgotten."

He cleared his throat and moved a little away from her. "Susan, I've got two kids. I've been married for fifteen years now. And, and—"

"And what?"

"I've never been unfaithful to my wife."

She laughed. "You poor guy," she said.

Even in the dark, she could tell that he was fiercely clenching the windowsill. She knew that all she had to do was reach out and touch him on the small of the back. Then he would turn to her. Her wrist was trembling. She was conscious of the power of her hand.

"I'm happy," he said.

Her eyes filled with tears. She remembered her agony after they had parted the last time. But she had been over that pain for twenty years! Why was she experiencing it again?

She put her forehead against the glass. Her life had been a seesaw of happiness and despair, but she had always been able to put the past behind her and pick herself up and go on to the next thing. When her life with Julian fell to pieces, she had turned to David. Later she had married Roger, and when she could no longer bear his infidelities, she had divorced him, too, and never looked back.

She stared out at the blizzard. There seemed to be nothing outside the window except blinding wind and snow. But what would have happened if she'd refused to let Nick leave her all those years ago? If she'd dropped out of school and followed him to Boston, instead of suffering for months, and then recovering so completely that Nick had been buried under twenty years of indifference?

Now she could go away and bury him again, this time for good. That's what he wanted her to do. He wanted her to again make him a meaningless figure in her life. All she had to do was turn and walk back down those dark stairs.

For half a minute, the wind dropped, and Susan glimpsed the whole length of the street, every visible object—cars, mailboxes, fence posts—decorated with snow. Then with a howl that shook the glass her forehead was touching, a gust blew the world out of her sight. She felt a moment of terror.

She put her hand on the small of Nick's back, right where she used to put it, and with a moan he turned to face her, his mouth on hers. She led him to the bare mattress.

My Death

When my mother's Italian family came to visit, I stayed in the kitchen with my stepfather. He had been a ship's baker in the Merchant Marine during the Second World War, and now worked in a bakery on Greenmount Avenue. He smelled of yeast, and there was always flour under his fingernails. We read the Sunday paper together at the chipped enamel table, trying to ignore the commotion from the front room, where my frightening grandparents, who spoke as much Italian as English, were shouting at my mother or one of my uncles or at each other.

My father had been killed in an accident down on the docks where he had gone to work as a welder after his return from the South Pacific. I was so young that I only had a single memory of him. When I closed my eyes, and concentrated, I could see a tall, black-haired man spinning the globe in the hall, and pointing to a speck in the big blue part where he said he had fought during the war. Later, I used to look for the speck, but I could never find it again. My mother had married Lyle, a widower and friend of my father, when I was four. I vaguely remembered the wedding. At first Lyle had slept in my mother's bedroom, but now he had a twin bed and a chest of drawers in the basement. When I grew up, the arrangement seemed strange to me. But at the age of seven I took it for granted. The basement belonged to Lyle. The upstairs belonged to my mother.

The kitchen, though, was a no-man's-land. My mother cooked all the meals while Lyle read the newspaper page by page, smoked, coughed, hummed to himself, and occasionally, when I coaxed him on his day off, made cream puffs or éclairs. Sometimes Lyle would go down to the bar in his ancient Ford, and come back with a basket of steamed crabs. Then my mother would spread newspapers over the kitchen table, and we would eat crabs until our fingers were sore and we were so stuffed we could hardly move. My mother would drink a beer, the only time she ever drank, and Lyle would let me finish his bottles. I liked to go out into the backyard afterwards, my head spinning from the beer, and lie in the grass. It was a narrow yard, divided from the other row-house yards by a picket fence, but behind the yard were the forested grounds of an orphanage. I could hear the distant shouts of the orphan children playing in the dusk, and it seemed to me that I was a lucky boy.

My grandparents visited us every third or fourth Sunday, rotating their visits among their other married children. My unmarried aunt, Dominica, and my two huge bachelor uncles, Luigi and Gabe, came with them. My mother, who was beginning to grow stout herself, always dressed two chickens and made a cake from a mix.

Lyle and I ate in the kitchen. We had just finished our cake on one such Sunday when my mother burst through the door. Her face was mottled, and her black hair, streaked with grey, was standing out from her head, as if she had been tearing at it.

"What carrying on!" she cried. "And Mama keeps getting worse."

"What's wrong with her?" asked Lyle.

"They took her to the doctor last week. They're doing tests, but she says she knows she's dying. She wants us to send her body back to Sicily. It would cost a fortune! And Papa won't shut up about the farm. First he's giving it to one of us, then another. And he told Mama he'd throw her down the well if she didn't shut up about Palermo." She clenched her fists in the air. "I know he's my papa, but he's so mean. Why does he have to be so mean?"

"Concetta! Concetta!" my grandfather's deep, roaring voice called from the other room.

My mother went running. Lyle sighed and folded up his section of the paper. I handed him the comics, but he shook his head.

"Where will you be buried, Lyle?" I asked.

He laughed, narrowing his eyes. It was hot, and he had rolled up his shirtsleeves. I could see the blue and red tattoos on his upper arms. Sometimes I had him flex his muscles for me, and then he reminded me of Popeye. One tattoo was a heart with a snake twisted through it. The other was an anchor.

"Bury me at sea," Lyle said. "Row me out and toss me over."

"How far out?" I asked. I looked at his face, stubbled with grey beard. His pale blue eyes were looking off in the distance. I couldn't tell if he was serious or not.

"Till you can't see land," he said. "Then toss me in for the sharks—and the mermaids." He winked.

"Joey!" my mother called. "Come here! Your grandfather wants to see you."

I got up from the table reluctantly. My mother's family had left the dining-room table, which was covered with dirty plates, chicken bones, crumpled napkins, and water glasses with visible marks from greasy lips, and had moved into the stifling front room. The heavy curtains were drawn against the hot July sun, and the end-table lamps were burning. My aunt

Dominica, in a flowered pink dress, took up most of the sofa. My grandmother, who had recently lost a lot of weight, was leaning against the corner of the sofa, her eyes closed. Her face was drawn and grey. Luigi was in his undershirt, his olive-colored arms glistening with sweat. He was so fat he seemed to have breasts, and I was always too shy to look at him directly. He was shaking his fist at my grandfather, shouting and cursing. He shut his mouth abruptly when he saw me. My uncle Gabe was sitting on the hassock. His face was red, and he was chewing angrily on the tip of his thick mustache. My grandfather sat in the armchair, leaning forward, his hands on his knees. His black eyes gleamed in his withered brown face.

"Come here, Joey!" he growled when he saw me. When I came close enough, he reached out and grabbed me by the upper arm.

"This is my boy," he muttered. "This is my grandson. I'm going to take him back to the farm with me. He's going to live with me and the rest of you can go to hell. To hell, do you hear!" His voice rose. "I hate all your guts!"

A wave of fear passed over me. I disliked my grandparents' farm, and lately my mother had given up trying to coax me into going with her when she visited. They lived in a huge, ramshackle house without indoor plumbing. At night I had to use a chamber pot which was kept under the bed, and in the daytime, I had to cross a yard full of chickens to get to the outhouse. My grandmother made me feed the chickens, and I was never quick enough. They would fly up in my face for corn until I ran screaming. Then I was put to work nailing boards in the fence, scrubbing the porch, shelling peas, weeding the garden. My mother told me, when I was older, that her parents had taken her out of school when she was in sixth grade, and put her to work cleaning house. Her father used to beat her shoulders with a switch, or hit her on the side of the head. I had never been hit, but the constant shouting in my grandparents' house made me sick to my stomach.

"He can't," my mother said. "He goes to school."

"I'm going to leave the farm to Joey," my grandfather said. "I've made up my mind."

Luigi made a disgusted noise. I felt there was malice in the way that Gabe was looking at me.

"I don't want it," I said faintly, but Dominica had begun to shout and no one heard me.

"You can't deny your own flesh and blood!" Dominica screamed. "Luigi is the oldest. And Mario's got three kids— two boys, just as good as Joey!"

"Ha!" my grandfather laughed. He pulled me closer.

Then my mother screamed piercingly. "Oh, Mama, what's wrong!"

My grandmother's head had fallen to one side. She was gasping for breath. Dominica wailed, and my grandfather let go my arm. I backed away. My mother ran for the bottle of Mogen David which she kept on the sideboard, and returned with a juice glass full of wine. She put her hand behind my grandmother's head and tried to get her to drink.

"Unbutton her dress," Gabe said. "She needs air."

"Get the fan from upstairs, Joey," my mother called.

My grandmother's eyes had opened. "I dreamed I was in heaven," she said. "I saw a flock of sheep just like the ones we had at home in Sicily." She pushed the wine away. I ran into the hall and up the narrow stairs to my mother's bedroom, where she kept a small fan on the dresser. I unplugged it and brought it down. As soon as Luigi took it from me, I ran back upstairs to my own room and shut the door. I was trembling.

I looked around my small bedroom. The wallpaper, covered with large, salmon-pink roses, was beginning to peel and crack, and my mother had promised to buy me some cowboy wallpaper. I already had curtains printed with cowboys roping steers, and brandishing six-shooters. I kept my toys on the top bunk bed, and slept on the lower one. My toy train was in a box under the bed, and my library books were stacked on the top of my bookcase. It had never occurred to me before that I could be taken away from this room, away from my mother.

The air was heavy and still. I went over to the window and opened it all the way. I could see the third-floor dormer windows of the orphanage above the treetops, and I thought about all the children who lived over there. Once upon a time they had lived happily at home.

I felt tears in my eyes. I looked down at the dark green grass of my backyard, at the tomato plants Lyle had staked up, and at the row of zinnias along the fence. One of my shirts was hanging on the clothesline, beside two of Lyle's bakery aprons, which were stiff with starch.

It was so quiet that I knew my grandparents had left. I went downstairs. My mother was washing dishes, muttering to herself, and I slipped past her. Lyle was sitting on the back step, smoking. In a few hours, in the middle of the night, he had to go to the bakery and start mixing dough in huge vats.

I walked down the yard and stepped on something hard. I searched the grass and found one of my green rubber soldiers, a little featureless man in a helmet, and stuck him in my pocket. The sun was setting, and the backyard was deep in shadow. I opened the gate and went into the mulberry-stained alley, which ran down between the rows of fenced yards and the orphanage grounds. Gnats rose out of the dense undergrowth, which smelled of decayed bark, and moss, and rank, wild spearmint. Hidden in the overgrown tangle was a barbed-wire fence, but I knew a place where other children had twisted back the wire to get into the orphanage grounds. I had never done more than poke my shoulders through the hole, but this evening I felt compelled to go through it. I wanted to feel what it was like to be an orphan. I waded through deep, feathery grass, pushed back some vines and briars, and stooped through thorny brambles which tore at my bare arms before I reached a clearing in the forest where I could stand upright and catch my breath.

I heard a child shouting not far away. I walked cautiously over crackling pine needles. The shout came again. It was so dark in the forest that when I came to a wide sweep of lawn, I was dazzled by the light from the pink sky where the sun was setting. At first I was only aware of the big red brick building across the lawn, with its odd slate roof and long verandah. The top row of windows still reflected the sun. I spotted a sundial in the middle of the lawn, and had just taken a step in that direction when two children burst out of the trees and came running toward me.

The older boy was chasing the younger. They both had shaved heads. The younger boy, who was about my age, was gasping for breath, holding his side; the older boy tackled him and pulled him to the ground. Then he began to pummel the younger boy with his fists, hitting his chest and head over and over again. They were only a few feet away from me, but so intent on each other that neither saw me. The younger boy began to sob and howl, but the older one kept up his blows. Blood began to flow from the boy's nose. I was paralyzed. I could neither run away nor cry out.

Then a girl came running across the lawn, shouting something. The older boy stopped his blows. In a single snake-like movement, he twisted away from his victim, leapt up, and hurried off along the edge of the trees. In a moment the younger boy, holding his bloody nose, got to his feet, too. He seemed to waver. I thought he was going to fall, but then he, too, ran off in the same direction. I was startled by how fast he was able to run after such punishment.

The girl must have spotted me from some distance. She veered to the left and came running straight toward me. She had red, stringy hair, and was wearing a faded print dress with sleeves that were too short for her long, bony arms. She stopped running abruptly, right in front of me. We stared at each other for a moment while she caught her breath. I was afraid to run, for she looked like she could easily catch me. She had a pale, freckled face, small, light-blue eyes, and a large, greenish bruise on her forehead.

"Who are you?" she asked in a harsh voice. "You don't live at the Home."

"I live back there," I said nervously, gesturing to the trees behind me. The girl was three or four years older than me. She wasn't smiling, and I felt my heart pounding. "Are you an orphan?" I asked in a polite voice.

She blinked at me. Her lashes were pale and short. She looked to the left and right, then back at my face. "What's that?"

"It means your mother and father are dead."

She scratched her neck. "My ma's dead, I guess. But my pa ain't dead."

I looked at the big building behind her. The rosy glow on the bricks was beginning to fade. It would be dark soon. "Then why do you live here?" I asked. "Why don't you live with your pa?"

"He's in prison," she said in a matter-of-fact voice. "He bashed my ma."

"He what?"

"He bashed her. He bashed her face open. Her face was all bloody. They were always fighting, and one day he bashed her good. I saw it. She just fell down dead, and her face was all bloody. So the police came."

"You mean he killed her?"

She laughed. "I said so. Hey, you got any neat toys? The toys here are crap. Those kids I was after just broke the arm off my doll. I'm going to bash them good. You got anything for me?" The girl put her face down close to mine. She said in a wheedling voice, "Come on, you must have some neat toys. You could get me some."

Her breath was sour. I was afraid that any moment she would grab me with one of her large hands. Then she would bash me.

I reached into my pocket. "Here," I said, bringing out the soldier. "You can have this."

She took it eagerly. "Neat. You got some more?"

"At home."

Her hands clamped down on my shoulders. "You go get me some more," she said. "I'll wait here. We can be friends from now on."

"All right," I said in a shaky voice.

"Promise."

"I promise."

"I'll find you if you don't come back," she said. "I'll beat you up."

She let me go, and I dashed back into the woods. It took me a long time to find the opening in the barbed wire again, and when I got back to my own yard it was almost completely dark. Lyle had gone inside. My mother was putting the last dishes away.

"Aren't you going to lock the back door?" I asked.

"I never lock it," she said. "Lyle doesn't have a key to the back door."

I stared at the door. I could only hope that the red-haired girl had not followed me. If I never played in the backyard again, she would not know which house I lived in.

I slept fitfully. In one dream my grandfather had me by the arm, and was pulling me into the barn toward the stall of an enormous mule, which was rearing and kicking. In another dream, I woke up and thought I wasn't dreaming. A woman with a bloody face was standing near the closet, gesturing to me. Then I was really awake. I saw that the closet door was wide open, and a breeze was causing my bathrobe, which was hanging on a hook, to flap back and forth.

I heard thunder. Then rain began. I got up and took a sip of water from the glass on my dresser, and went over to close the window. But the rain was falling straight down, and I leaned on the windowsill, looking out. When lightning flashed, I could see the serrated top of the orphanage. The fir trees swept restlessly back and forth. The rain and the trees combined to make a loud, whispering noise, and I felt I was being spoken to. "She's going to bash you," whispered the firs. "She's going to bash you," sang the rain as it pinged on the neighbor's awning, and pattered on the sidewalk. The thunder was like deep, distant laughter. I put my hands over my ears, then pressed my ear flaps with my fingers. Now the whispering seemed to be inside my head. I dived back into bed, covering my head with my blanket.

I must have fallen asleep at last, for when I opened my eyes, it was sunny. I felt better, but while I was eating my cereal I remembered that I could not go out in the backyard anymore, and the thought made me sad. I spent the next few days playing desultorily on the front porch.

One day, about a week later, I was sitting on the top step, blowing soap bubbles through a metal wand, when the red-haired girl came jumping rope down the sidewalk. She spotted me at once.

She came up to the porch, tying her rope around her waist. "I knew I'd find you," she said. "Where are those soldiers you said you'd give me?"

I dropped the wand back into my glass bottle of bubbles, and screwed the lid on tight. "I can't play," I said.

"Give me that," she said. Before I could move out of her range, she twisted my wrist. She pulled the jar of bubbles out of my hand. "Now listen," she said, sitting down beside me. "I can beat anyone up, you hear? But I want us to be friends. Now you go get me some of them soldiers."

"My mom won't let me," I said.

"Just don't tell her." The girl lifted her skirt, and pointed to a large bruise on her thigh. "I got this yesterday. I had to bash this kid. I waited for him in the bushes. My, it hurt."

"Did he kick you?"

She nodded. "But I kicked him back good." She swung her foot, in its battered brown oxford, in my direction. "I could kick you," she said in a low voice. "But I won't."

I felt faint.

"Go on," she said.

I got up and went inside. Lyle was gone, but I could hear my mother in the kitchen. She might be able to chase the girl away, but I knew I wouldn't be safe. I would have to stay in the house forever, and that wasn't possible. In the fall I had to walk six blocks to school. The girl would find me and beat me up. She would bash my face.

I went up to my room and gathered a handful of my soldiers. I picked the ones I liked the least, the ordinary ones that only marched. I shoved the ones that crouched over machine guns or fit into tanks into the back of my underwear drawer.

When I handed them over, the red-haired girl stuffed the soldiers into her pocket, along with my bottle of bubbles. She stood up, twirling one end of her rope.

"I'll come back tomorrow afternoon. We'll play some more," she said. "You can bring me another toy."

"I can't play tomorrow."

"You'd better." She jabbed me hard with her shoe. "You'd just better. What's your name, kid? I'll knock on the door and get you."

"Joey," I said faintly.

"I'm Martha." She ran down the front walk, then turned around. She waved. "I'll see you tomorrow, Joey."

That night I looked around my room to see what I could part with most easily. I couldn't give Martha my bear, even though its paw was torn. I had lots of trucks. One had a broken wheel, and I dug it out of my toy box in the closet. But a long time ago it had been my favorite truck. I put it gently back beside a can of Lincoln logs. I looked at my bookcase. Now that I had learned to read, I knew the picture books were for babies, but I still liked to look at them when I was alone.

I decided to give Martha my yo-yo, but when I held it in my hand, I couldn't do it. I had won it at a party playing pin the tail on the donkey. I put it back in the toy box. I closed my eyes and reached out blindly toward the bookcase, pulling out the first book that my fingers touched. It was *Black Beauty*.

The next afternoon, I waited for Martha on the porch, *Black Beauty* on my knees. I waited all afternoon, but she never came. Once my mother asked me what I was doing, and I told her I was reading. I watched two ants fighting over a crumb in the grass. Cars roared past on Argonne Drive. Children came pedaling by on bicycles, but there was no sign of Martha. Finally my mother called me in to supper.

She did not come the next day either. On the third day I stayed inside playing with my train set, feeling happier than I had in a long time.

"Joey," my mother called up the stairs. "There's a girl here to play with you."

The news made me shudder. I turned off the transformer, and my engine came to a stop. I grabbed *Black Beauty*, and jumped over the tracks which covered my bedroom floor. Martha was waiting for me on the porch. She had a fresh scratch on her face.

"They locked me up, the bastards," she said. "That's why I couldn't come those other days."

"Why did they do that?"

"I don't know why. Something I did, I guess. Some kid told. I'll get him, though." She was sitting on the green metal lawn chair where my mother liked to sit in the evening, swinging her legs back and forth. She had scabs on both her knees. "What did you bring me?"

"Here," I said, handing her the book.

She opened her eyes in surprise. Then she took the book from me and flung it in my face. It hit the bridge of my nose, then tumbled to the ground; some of the pages ripped.

I held my nose. "Hey!" I cried.

"I don't want no books," she said fiercely. "I can't even read." She jumped up, and grabbed my arm. "Come on, let's go into your house. You take me to your room, and I'll find what I want."

She already had the screen door open. She shoved me into the hall. "Where is it?" she whispered. "We don't want your ma to hear."

"Upstairs," I said.

She gave me a push, and I led her upstairs to my room. She shut the door behind us.

"A train set," she said, her eyes gleaming. "That's what I want!" She knelt down beside the engine. "Wow. This is great."

"You can't have that," I said. "Lyle bought me that. He won on the numbers, and he bought me that special."

She looked up at me, frowning. "You said I could have anything I wanted. Well, this is what I want, kid. I want this train."

"No," I said.

She ignored me. The box I kept the train set in was sitting on the lower bunk. She put the engine into the box, then uncoupled the other cars and the caboose. She pulled the pieces of track apart, and tossed them on top. Finally she wedged the transformer into the box and closed the flaps. I watched her in horror. Nothing belonged to me now. She would take everything and I couldn't stop her.

When she was done, she glanced at the books in my bookcase. "My. Look at all them books. Can you read, kid?"

"Yes," I said numbly.

She frowned. She seemed to be thinking. Then she reached in her dress somewhere and pulled out a folded piece of blue-ruled notebook paper. "Read this to me then. It's a letter from Pa. I didn't want any of them at the Home to read it to me."

She handed me the paper, which felt slick and greasy. The creases were worn, as if it had been opened and refolded many times.

"*Dear Marty,*" I read.

"He calls me Marty," she said. "I'm really Martha."

"*Dear Marty. This guy I know says he'll write down what I say. I'm real sorry about your Ma. She shouldn't ought have said that, though—*"

"She called him a dirty liar," Martha interrupted. "That's when he bashed her."

I cleared my throat, and continued. "*I miss you a lot. It stinks in here. I been in a lot of. . . .*" I peered at the messy word. "I think it says *fights.*"

"Go on," Martha said eagerly.

"*But some of the guys is nice. I sure am lonely. I miss the woods and the . . . sill?*" I questioned. "What's that?"

"Still. My pa makes the best white lightning in western Maryland."

"What's that?"

She laughed. "Go on reading."

"*I miss you a lot, honey. When you grow up I hope you come visit me—less I'm dead. Your loving Pa. The end.*"

I handed the letter back. She refolded it carefully. "I sure am lonely, too. I sure hate Baltimore. We used to live out where it was cool and nice, with birds and cows and big hills, and sweet corn to eat, and chicken pie."

Then she shook herself. "I've got to go. Open the door, kid."

I opened the door of my room while she picked up the box that contained my train in both arms. I followed her downstairs. My mother was just hanging up the phone in the hall, and saw us. She looked like she had been crying, but the sight of Martha caused her to quickly control her face.

"Where are you going, Joey? Isn't that your train set?"

"Outside," I said lamely.

"I told you not ever to take that train outside, didn't I?" She grabbed the box out of Martha's arms. "Now you go out and say good-bye to your friend, Joey. Then I want to talk to you about something."

My mother carried the box upstairs. Martha scowled after her. We went out on the porch, and I tried not to show her how happy I was.

"What a bitch," Martha said. "All right, Joey. You listen now, or you'll be sorry. You'll have to give it to me piece by piece. First I want the engine. You bring the engine out here tomorrow. You have that engine for me tomorrow, or I'll choke you dead."

I stared at her freckled, intent face. She had large, strong hands, and I believed her. Now I wished she had just taken the whole train. Losing it piece by piece, under such a threat, seemed much worse to me. I fought back tears.

Martha grabbed the front of my shirt. She shook me, and I felt as if my brain were sliding around in my head. Then she let me go.

"You swear?"

"I swear."

"You better," she hissed. "I can find you anywhere. I'll leave you dead in the bushes."

She ran down the street. I went back inside. My mother was in the front room, sobbing loudly into her sleeve. She looked up when she heard me. "Your grandmother had a heart attack," she said. "She's gone to heaven, Joey."

My mother went away that night to help with funeral arrangements, and Lyle made tuna salad for supper. He added pickles and olives and eggs to it, and left out the celery. One of his tomatoes was ripe and we ate it. He let me have a half a can of beer.

"Were you ever scared someone was going to kill you?" I asked when I had drunk some of my beer.

He screwed up his eyes. "Kill me? Well, let me see. There was this big bruiser on the *Ariadne* once who used to threaten everyone. I was the cook's helper, and this fellow didn't like the taste of my coffee. He said he'd kill me if it didn't get any better." Lyle laughed. "I poured a little shoe polish in his coffee. That made it black enough all right."

I woke up in the middle of the night. I thought I heard someone laugh, but I must have been dreaming. Or perhaps my mother had cried out. I went to the window and looked out. I saw Martha standing in the middle of Lyle's tomato patch, looking up at my room. But her huddled figure was ragged and indistinct, and when the moon came out from behind a cloud, I couldn't see her anymore. Either she had slipped away or she had never been there.

The next morning my mother told me to put on my new pants and shirt, and wash my face.

"We're going out to the farm to say good-bye to your grandmother," she said. She was standing in the hall in her slip, and I saw her good navy-blue dress spread out on the bed in her room. She had deep, pouchy circles under her eyes.

"I can't," I said, shivering as I thought of Martha. "I've got to stay here."

"Do I have to dress you like a baby?" my mother said irritably. "Hurry up."

I went back into my room and took my brown pants off a hanger. There was no hope for me now. Martha was going to kill me. Tomorrow or the next day or the day after, my mother would insist that I go to the corner store, or over to my Aunt Mary's, three blocks away. Martha would be waiting. She wouldn't listen to any excuses. She would choke me to death and leave me dead in the bushes.

I buttoned my white shirt, and then my mother came in and put the cuff links through the holes. As I stood there, conscious of her roughened fingers on my wrists, I knew I was dying. It was not an unpleasant feeling. I seemed to be numb and light-headed at the same time.

Lyle looked strange and miserable in his old pin-striped suit. The shoulders were heavily padded, and his whole figure was distorted. He had rubbed some sweet-smelling lotion into his hair, which made it slick and flat on his head.

He made me some toast, but it tasted like straw. Then we left. I sat in the backseat of the car. I looked out the window at the Baltimore streets, and the long rows of red brick houses that looked just like mine went by in a blur. Soon we were out in the country. The trees were drooping and dusty in the hot, still air.

Cars were parked all over the scraggly lawn in front of my grandparents' farmhouse. I could hear the rooster, and the shouts of the men who were gathered on the porch, but the sounds seemed faraway. I followed my mother and Lyle. My uncle Gabe and my uncle Luigi and my uncle Mario were on the porch, sweating in their dark suits, along with several other men, cousins or in-laws, whom I didn't recognize. They were all swearing and shouting. My grandfather was roaring.

"You're all bastards," he screamed at his sons. "Ungrateful pigs!"

"Oh, Papa," my mother cried.

"Go on in, Concetta," yelled my grandfather, directing his malevolent gaze at her for a moment. "Go on in and fight over the silverware with your sisters. I should have drowned you all at birth."

My mother sniveled, and wiped her eyes. She hurried into the house, while Lyle backed off, and went slyly around the corner toward the barn. I knew he was going to have a smoke and spend the day out of shouting range.

I hesitated. My grandfather, terrible as he was, represented my last hope of survival. If I agreed to live here at the farm, and never returned with my mother and Lyle, then Martha would not be able to kill me.

I squeezed between my uncle Mario and one of the strange men. No one noticed me. My grandfather had taken off his jacket, and the whole front of his white shirt was wet. His legs were spread apart, and he was gesturing wildly. Luigi and Gabe were face to face, shouting at each other.

"Swine! Swine!" my grandfather shouted. His sons ignored him. Gabe was holding a bottle of beer in a threatening way, as if he were going to smash it over Luigi's head.

I tugged at my grandfather's pants leg. "Grandpa, I want to live with you," I said in a voice that sounded tiny even to my own ears.

My grandfather swung his hand out blindly. He hit me on the side of the head with his palm, and I went sprawling across the porch.

"You're crazy, Pop!" Mario grabbed me up before I had barely hit the ground. He dragged me to the door. "Get out of here, Joey. Go find your mother. This is no place for you."

He shoved me inside. I was too stunned to cry. I held my ear until the pain began to subside, then walked down the familiar buckled linoleum of the hall to the parlor. I heard women howling and sobbing. I hesitated at the door. I smelled garlic in the house, and floor wax, but I could also smell something sweet and strange, which must be the smell of death.

My grandmother was dead. She was in heaven with the sheep, and soon I would be, too. She had known she was going to die. She couldn't save herself any more than I could.

Then I heard two women talking on the stair landing above me.

"You mean she just took the ring! Just took it off her dead finger! Oh, my God!"

"She said Mama wanted her to have it. She was going to take the silver gravy boat, too, but Dominica stopped her."

"I told you she was heartless. But what about Mama's watch? She promised that to me."

A door slammed. I couldn't hear the women's voices anymore, but I had another insight into my death. I'd better give my train set to Lyle right away, or Martha might sneak up to my room while I was lying dead in the bushes, and just take it. I knew she was heartless.

The parlor door opened.

"There you are, Joey." My mother pulled me inside. The sweet odor was even stronger. There were flowers everywhere. Lilies shone almost iridescently in the dim, heavily curtained room. Two women were crying noisily together on the sofa, which had been moved to the side of the room. My aunt Dominica was alternately sobbing and shouting "Mama! Mama!" while a thin nun in a white veil patted her hand.

A blue metal coffin made the furniture in the room look small and unimportant. My mother drew me toward it.

"Come say good-bye to your grandmother, Joey."

At first I resisted. I wanted to see my death, but I was terrified. I pulled away from my mother.

"Don't be afraid, little boy," the nun said in a soft, whispery voice. "Your grandmother is with God now. She's very beautiful."

I allowed my mother to lift me up to look at my grandmother. There was a hole in the lid of the coffin for her face to show. She was resting on a lace pillow. Her lips and cheeks were red and waxy-looking. Her eyes were shut.

I stared at her intently until my mother set me back down on the carpet.

"He looks like his grandmother, doesn't he?" the nun said to my mother. "What's his name?"

"Don't say that," my mother said, a little sharply. She didn't like nuns. "His name's Joey."

"Ah, Joseph," the nun said sweetly.

The rest of the day was dreamlike. I remember eating potato salad in the kitchen and drinking lemonade. The hearse came, and all the cars followed it out to the country cemetery where my grandmother was buried against her wishes, and against the wishes of Luigi, who had bought a grave plot in a new Baltimore cemetery. My grandfather cried and threw his arms around the coffin before it was lowered down into the hole. I felt myself going down into the hole with my grandmother, and I pressed my face against my mother's arm. Then we drove home in almost complete silence.

The next day, while my mother and Lyle were at the grocery store, I took my train set down to the basement. I placed it on Lyle's narrow bed. I remembered the delight in his eyes the day he brought it home for me, and put the track together. He liked to run the engine backwards.

Then I arranged my bear on my mother's pillow. After that, I looked around my room with indifference. I didn't care anymore. Martha could steal the rest, or my mother could give it to my cousins.

To save trouble, I put my good pants and shirt back on. I washed my face and hands. Then I went out on the porch and sat down in the lawn chair.

It wasn't long before I saw Martha. She was riding a blue bicycle with a straw basket on the handlebars. She pedaled up to the porch, jabbed down the kickstand with her foot, and jumped off.

"You little creep," she said. She put her hands on her hips. "I told you I wanted that engine yesterday."

I took a deep breath. I felt dizzy.

She came closer. "How do you like my new bike?" she asked, smirking. "I stole it in the park."

I pressed my lips tightly together.

"I'll give you one last chance," Martha said. "Bring me the engine or you're dead."

"I'm already dead," I said.

She frowned at me. "Don't make me mad."

I looked up at the blue sky for the last time. The clouds were white as sheep. I closed my eyes.

Martha slammed her fist into my face. Blood spurted from my nose. I opened my eyes, gasping, my mouth filled with blood. There was blood on my shirt.

"Get out of here, you nasty girl!" I heard Mrs. Pirrone, the woman next door, shouting above the roar in my ears.

I saw Martha leap on her bike. While she was jerking at the kickstand, Mrs. Pirrone hit her on the head with a broom. Then she picked me up and carried me into the kitchen to put wet towels on my face. My mother came in with a bag of groceries.

"A big, nasty girl!" Mrs. Pirrone shouted excitedly. "I went out to sweep the porch, and there she was, slugging Joey. I've seen her around. But Joey's all right. It's just a nosebleed. And he never even cried, Concetta!"

The orphanage was closed that fall. The building no longer met fire-code regulations, and the children were sent to foster homes. I never saw Martha again. I used to dream about her, though. I'd look out my window in the middle of the night, and imagine she was standing near the picket fence, or among the tomato plants, waiting to kill me. But when I grew up, I knew I'd never die that handsomely.

The Cat and the Clown

—I lived the life of a cat until I was nineteen, Vicki said.

We were all sitting in a booth at the Dream Cafe telling stories about our first lovers. She'd just been listening up until now, and it was her turn. We knew she had lots to tell. She had long, straight, chestnut hair and strong bones. Men turned their heads to look at her.

—Are you changing the subject? Laurie asked.

Vicki shook her head. I was just trying to remember what it was like before sex, she said. It was like being a cat.

—A spayed cat, somebody laughed.

—Yes, a house cat, Vicki said. Curled up most of the time. Stretching. Looking out windows. Eating muffins.

—Muffins!

—Why not muffins? Olivia said. My cat used to love powdered-sugar doughnuts.

Martha wiped the foam of beer off her upper lip.

—My mother's cat—his name was Dirt-Boy—loved to lick the olives in martinis. He'd sit there waiting until she was done with her drink. He liked pretzels, too.

—Dirt-Boy? That was the name of your mother's cat? Vicki asked.

—Yeah, his nickname. He liked to roll in the dirt.

—My mother's cat was called Gingernut, Vicki said.

—We're getting way, way off the subject. Laurie looked at Vicki. Go on.

—Well, I was a cat, and then I wasn't. I remember looking in the bathroom mirror. I'd turned into a big, tall girl with breasts, and hips, and a scary mouth that wanted to be kissed all the time.

A fork clattered to the floor at another booth, and we all turned to watch a guy with grizzled hair reach down to pick it up. We'd seen him around before, but didn't know his name.

The Dream Cafe was divided into three sections. Sometimes we sat up front in the family part, where minors were allowed. If we sat there, we drank cappuccino. Tonight we were in the smoky bar section, and we were all drinking drafts. At night they showed foreign movies in the back room, and if we didn't feel like talking much, we'd gather back there, where you could sip something strong if you liked, or not even drink at all.

—How did it happen? Laurie leaned forward. She had short, dark hair and rimless glasses. She was a law student, and felt an obligation to keep things focused.

Vicki stretched back in her chair, half-closing her eyes.

—I think I could have gone on forever without an interior life if I hadn't fallen in love with a clown. She laughed a little ruefully, and took a sip of her beer. You know, I wish I were still a cat.

—But you're not, Laurie said. Go on. And do you mean a real clown, or is that just an adjective?

—Sort of both, Vicki said.

She squeezed her eyes together tightly, then opened them wide. Now they seemed glazed and faraway, as if they were no longer reflecting the rest of us sitting around her. We had vanished.

She began.

—I've always hated clowns. I can't explain why. My older brother, Johnny, hated them too, and he was always teasing me. We had this little game that got more and more out of hand over the years. One Christmas when I was twelve and he was seventeen, I opened a package from him, and there was this clown doll with orange hair. A few days later, I snuck the clown doll into his bed, so he'd find it when he turned back the covers. Not long afterwards, the clown doll showed up again in my bed with a love sonnet scotch-taped to its tummy. Then I sent Johnny a clown birthday card; about a month later I found a clown coloring book in my book bag when I got to school.

—This sort of thing went on for years, even after he'd moved out to his own apartment. It's amazing how many clown products there are. Johnny and I found them all, and gave them to each other on every possible occasion. Clown bubble bath, clown bubble gum, clown coffee mugs, wind-up clowns, clown barrettes, books about clowns, inflatable clowns—you name it. And then the other half of the game was to hide the horrible clown thing in the other's place, which was easier for Johnny, because I still lived at home and he could stop by when I wasn't there. It was a lot harder for me to find excuses to go over to his apartment. Once I managed to get the inflatable clown into the driver's seat of his car when he was warming it up outside on a cold night. That was one of my biggest triumphs.

—After I graduated from high school, I started going downtown to the university. One of my friends threw a nineteenth-birthday party for me. She invited a bunch of our old friends who were back home for Christmas break. She also invited Johnny, because she had a crush on him, but he refused when he heard it was going to be all girls.

—Of course I knew I was going to get a clown gift from Johnny. It was just a matter of what, and when. But I thought I was pretty safe at the party. All the presents seemed to be from my friends, though of course Johnny might have talked one of them into wrapping something up for him as a joke.

But at least the cake was covered with blue and pink roses. One year I'd had to cut slices out of a frosted clown face.

—Around nine o'clock, just as I was opening the last present, a big oversized T-shirt with a cat on the front—everyone knew I was crazy about cats—the doorbell rang.

—Some of the girls went to the door. The rest of us heard a squeal, then peals of laughter.

—A huge, live clown walked into the room.

Vicki paused. The waitress was hovering over us. She was new at the Dream Cafe, and Vicki cleared her throat self-consciously.

—Anything else here? the waitress asked. She had a soft, educated voice. A long braid of dark hair fell down her back. She wore a lot of mascara and her lips were brightly painted. Her name tag said "Chloe."

—Another draft, Martha said.

—Make that two, Olivia added. Can you bring us some chips and cheese dip, too, please?

The new waitress moved off. Olivia was looking at her critically.

—Did you see those suede heels? She's not going to last long waitressing in those.

—She looks sad, Martha said. Don't you think so?

—Just tired, Olivia said. I used to work here, you know. After a while, you get so tired you can't feel your body anymore.

Laurie made a brushing gesture in the air, as if to wipe away all our remarks.

—OK, Vicki, you were talking about the clown at the door. What kind of clown? The hobo type like Emmett Kelly?

—No, no, the other kind. Vicki looked fierce. He had orange hair, a sad white face with big red lips, a huge nose, a baggy polka-dot costume and oversized feet. He carried one of those squeeze horns, too, and a big handful of balloons.

—Ugh, said Martha. I don't like clowns either.

—So, anyway, he comes into the living room followed by my girlfriends, and they're just rolling with laughter. Of course they all know about Johnny and me. Then he pulls a child's slate out of one of his pockets, and writes in chalk:

Where's the birthday girl?

—Everyone laughed and pointed at me. I laughed, too, but I was angry, and I could feel myself flushing. Johnny had really gone too far this time.

—The clown handed me the bouquet of balloons, then started playing "Happy Birthday" on a harmonica. My girlfriends started singing along. Afterwards, everyone applauded. Then, before I realized what was happening, the clown leaned down—he was really tall—and gave me a kiss with those big red lips.

Martha made a face.

—On your cheek?

—On my lips, Vicki said. And do you know what I did?

She paused. The waitress had just returned with our beers and the basket of chips. We waited until she had set them in front of Martha and Olivia, and made a notation on the green bill underneath the napkin holder.

—What did you do? Olivia asked in a low voice as the waitress left.

—I cried. I broke down and cried.

—Jesus, Laurie said. And what about the poor clown?

—The clown just stepped back like he'd been slapped. Then he started apologizing in a normal man's voice. He'd been hired by my brother. He was a semiprofessional clown, and he was hired to play "Happy Birthday" he said, give me a birthday kiss, and then entertain us all for an hour with his clown act. Now he felt terrible.

—My girlfriends all took his side at once, and told me to lighten up. So I did. I swallowed the lump in my throat, winked back my tears, and tried to act normal and cheerful. The clown did his clown act—he squeezed his horn, squirted water out of his buttonhole flower, all the stuff they do—and I sat there with the others, pretending I thought it was funny, and applauding when it was over. But I hated it. And when the clown left, he came over and took my hand in his big white glove. He pantomimed that he was sorry about the kiss. Then he squeezed my hand. He pulled out his slate again and wrote:

I'll call you soon.

—And did he? Olivia held a chip in the air.

—Of course he did, Laurie laughed. That's the whole point of the story. Go on, Vicki.

—He called me for a date the next day. I said no. I was sure Johnny had put him up to it anyway. Then one afternoon in January, when I got home from class, there he was in the house having coffee with my mother and Johnny.

—In his clown costume? Olivia asked.

Vicki shook her head.

—He was wearing blue jeans and a sweatshirt. I didn't even know who he was at first. I just saw this hunk sitting on the couch across from my mother.

—So he was good-looking? Laurie nodded.

—Not just good-looking, Vicki said emphatically. He was gorgeous. A dream guy—tall, wavy black hair, big shoulders. But he was awfully shy, and every time I looked at him, he flushed to the eyeballs. It turned out that was why he'd gone to clown school.

—You mean you can go to clown school? Jesus, Martha said with a shudder.

—Apparently a lot of people *want* to be clowns, Vicki said. And you can learn how to be one. They teach you how to put on makeup, create your own character, and do clown-type things like ride tricycles and perform mime. Chris—that was his name—always wanted to be a clown. When he was a clown, he lost his inhibitions, he said. It was a kind of therapy. Besides, he loved it.

—So you liked him, Laurie said.

Vicki nodded. My mother fixed me a cup of coffee, Johnny left, and I sat there talking with Chris. I loved the way he couldn't quite look at me, but when he did, his eyes were all shiny. Once Gingernut, our cat, came into the room and started to walk over the back of the couch, and I saw Chris stiffen up. Cats made him anxious, he said, but when I told him I loved cats, he started petting Gingernut, and after that, whenever he was over and the cat came into the room, he made a point of stroking her and calling her "pretty kitty" even though you could tell he didn't really like touching her.

Vicki finished her beer, but kept staring down into her glass.

—I know I've made it all sound really funny so far, she said, but Chris and I started going out, and it wasn't long before we were both in love. He was a sweet guy, really shy and kind and nervous around people. But he was so handsome that other girls would practically turn around on the street to look at him. I have to admit I really liked that. I was nineteen and I hadn't had many boyfriends—and none I really felt anything like love for. Chris was the first.

—What did he do when he wasn't a clown? Olivia asked.

—Oh, he was Johnny's age. He'd already finished college and worked as a systems analyst. He made good money, and had a nice apartment. I used to tell my parents that I was staying over at Johnny's, but I'd really spend the night with Chris. I started taking the pill, and we made love. At first I was uptight, but after a while I relaxed and it was wonderful. Chris knew exactly where to touch me. Afterwards, I loved to curl up next to him and put my head on his chest and fall asleep while he was reading and gently stroking me. I felt so warm and safe. I started imagining what it would be like to live together, to get married. I began to lose interest in school. It was hard to concentrate.

—But what about the clown business? Laurie asked.

—That was the thing, Vicki said. I just couldn't bear the fact that he was a clown, and I refused to ever see him in his costume or go to any of his clown things or even talk about it. Once I'd seen his polka-dot costume hanging in his closet with his suits, so I always made sure the closet door was shut after that. I was hoping of course that he'd give it up, but he said it was important to him, it was his way of expressing himself—it was like his art, he said. So on certain nights or especially Saturday afternoons, I knew he was off being a clown, and I tried not to think about it.

—Did your brother keep teasing you? Martha asked.

—No, he really liked Chris—they'd met through some mutual friends, it turns out—and he either sensed how serious things were between Chris and me or else Chris spoke to him about it and asked him to lay off. Anyway, the clown jokes stopped completely. It was just this hidden thing Chris and I never talked about.

—Once, I remember, it was the summer after we'd met, we went to the amusement park together and were having a great time. We were both soaked from the flume ride. Chris had won a blue teddy bear on the ringtoss, and I was holding a big pink cloud of cotton candy in one hand, and Chris's hand in the other, when suddenly this clown in a patchwork costume, who was selling balloons, came out of the crowd and started waving at us. Chris waved back.

—*It's Flim-Flam,* he said. *We met in clown school. She's a really good clown.*

—He started pulling me over to meet her, but I broke away and ran over to the Ferris wheel. The line was short, and I got on right away. When I looked down from my car at the top, I saw Chris with the blue bear under his arm talking to the clown.

—Don't you think you were going a little too far with the clown-avoidance thing? Laurie asked frowning.

—I know I was acting a little crazy, Vicki said, looking around for the waitress. I need another beer.

—There she is, Olivia said. She's talking to our man.

Olivia meant the man with the grizzled hair. He was about forty with interesting planes to his face. We liked to speculate about him.

—You could have talked to his friend, Laurie insisted. Even if she was a clown.

—Hey, I'm telling a story. Do I need to defend my actions, too? It's way in the past.

—I'm just trying to understand, Laurie said.

—Well, your reaction, Vicki sighed, was exactly Chris's reaction.

Olivia waved her hand over our heads.

—She's coming. Do you guys want another one, too?

—Sure, we all said.

—Another round of drafts, Olivia said. And another basket of chips.

The waitress smiled, and made a notation. She looked at Vicki. You know that guy over there, she said, he thinks he knows you from somewhere. He wanted to know if I knew you.

Vicki turned her head slightly to look. I've never seen him before, she said. She looked pleased.

—So Chris got mad at you, Laurie said, as soon as the waitress left.

—He was upset, Vicki said. He didn't say much, but he seemed moody on the way home. And when we got back to his place he confronted me. He told me that he loved me, but being a clown was part of his life, and I had to accept it. Just as he'd accepted the fact that I liked cats, and he didn't care for them much. And I had to admit it was true. He'd even given me a pair of cat earrings.

—We worked out a compromise. He was free to talk about being a clown, to tell me about his experiences, but I

didn't have to ever go with him or see him as a clown. And
for a while that seemed to work. But it was summer, and he
had more and more chances to be a clown—there were a lot
of children's birthday parties in backyards, and he started getting invitations from church groups and hospitals. He was
apparently one of the best clowns in the city. Something
about Chris's clown character appealed to everyone.

—Everyone who liked clowns to start with, Martha
said.

—Right, Vicki agreed.

—Did he have a special clown name? Laurie asked.

—Joujou, Vicki said. That's French baby talk for toy.

—Joujou the clown. Martha made a face.

—I had a summer job at a travel agency downtown, Vicki
said, and one Saturday evening I was hanging around waiting
for Chris. I knew he had to go to some clown thing that night,
but he'd said he would pick me up at six and drop me at home
so we could have a little time together.

—The car pulled up, and I ran out to get inside. But there
was a clown at the wheel. Chris was in his costume. No, I
shouted. I slammed the door shut, and ran down to the bus
stop. Chris was following me in the car, but the bus got there
first, and I jumped on. I was panting and almost crying.

—We were both angry at each other for about a week.
I felt betrayed, and he felt I was acting stupid—he even
got Johnny to try to talk to me about it, because he thought
the game Johnny and I had been playing for years had con-
tributed to my hysteria about clowns. That's what he called
it—hysteria.

—An ugly word. Martha nodded.

—He was so handsome, Vicki said. I loved playing soft-
ball with him in the park, or going bike riding, or out for pizza.
Other girls always turned around to look at us, and I knew
they were green with envy. But the idea of going around in
public with a clown, people turning their heads to look at us,

laughing not just at him, but at me, too—it made me cringe with shame.

—It sounds to me as if the problem was more with you than with him, Laurie said. Poor guy.

—Clowns are id figures, Martha said. I think they're creepy, too.

—Oh, for heaven's sake, Olivia laughed. Don't take sides. Let her finish.

—Do you want to hear this or not? Vicki was looking directly at Laurie.

Laurie looked away. I'm listening.

—It was a bad week for me. I really loved Chris, and I missed him terribly. And it was clear that everyone else was on his side—my parents, Johnny, even my girlfriends when I told them about it. Finally we made up. Chris said he loved me, too, and was almost ready to give up being a clown. But he just couldn't, he said. If he killed Joujou, it would be like killing himself. We went for a long walk around the lake, and we agreed that gradually—that was the word, gradually—steps had to be taken to get me over my phobia.

—Phobia! Martha shook her head.

Vicki took a long sip of her beer, then leaned forward determinedly.

—The idea was that I had to get used to Chris in the clown costume, she said. He thought it would be best if the occasion were a natural one for costumes. So we hit on Halloween. Some friends of his always had a party on Halloween. He would go as Joujou, and I would wear a costume, too. Everything would be natural and easy. The whole world would be in costume that night.

—I had a cat costume that I'd worn a few times before. It was pretty simple—black leotards, a sweatshirt hood with ears sewn onto it, a swishy cape and a black mask, long whiskers that I taped to my upper lip, and a yarn tail. I wore my tall black boots, too.

—All day I was nervous and dry-mouthed. Around six I got into my costume, and started pacing up and down the living room. My mother kept trying to calm me down, but she was sort of laughing at me, too. Underneath, she thought I was being silly. Then Chris knocked on the door—or rather, Joujou.

—He came into the living room, and my mother, who had never seen him as a clown before, admired him profusely. He honked his horn and did a few clown tricks for her, while I just stood there holding my cape together with one hand.

—*C'mon Vicki,* he said, reaching out for my hand with his white glove. *It's time to go.* His natural voice seemed strange coming out of the clown face, and for the first time I really looked at Joujou. He had a white face with red tears painted under eyes that gave the illusion of being stitched with thread. His red clown lips were painted in a wide circle around his real lips, and his putty nose was huge and mis-shapen.

—I followed him out to the car without a word. He took his white gloves off to drive, and the whole way over to the party I kept my eyes on his human hands gripping the wheel. I wouldn't look at his face, but I made a real effort to talk to him in a normal voice.

—Everyone was in costume at the party. There were gypsies and mummies and rock stars and witches and the usual assortment of Disney characters and spacemen, all dancing and drinking and talking together. But everyone *looked* like they were in costume, like they were just dressed up and pretending to be someone else, and it wasn't long before the monsters had taken off their hot rubber masks, and the gypsies had lifted their half-masks, and rolled them back across the tops of their heads. But Joujou didn't seem to be in costume. He seemed real, and every time we danced to a slow song I felt sweaty and cold when he held me against him.

—Once, when I went to the bathroom, I saw that my cat whiskers were missing. I didn't want to lose them, because they'd been pretty difficult to make, so I looked around for Chris. He was in the kitchen.

—*Chris*, I said, *was I wearing my whiskers when we danced the last time?*

—Instead of answering, he began to squeeze his horn and gesture, and I realized that he hadn't said a word all night. He was Joujou. He was only speaking in mime, or writing on his slate. Everyone in the kitchen was laughing. He pretended to stroke me as if I were a real cat. Then he made comic snipping motions with his bulky white fingers. He pulled my whiskers out of one of his voluminous pockets, and handed them to me with a flourish.

—I took the whiskers and turned to go. Suddenly I felt a tug. Joujou had me by the tail. Everyone was laughing hysterically. He pulled me back into the kitchen by my tail, and then my tail came off in his hand.

—I let him have the tail. I'd been drinking wine, but now I went over to the table where the drinks were set out and fixed myself a gin and tonic, heavy on the gin. I got drunker than I've ever been in my life.

—When the party ended, we went back to Chris's place. I was so drunk I was numb all over. I remember that he undressed me and started kissing me, but I was only semiconscious, more like a rag doll than a person. Once I opened my eyes and was aware of this scary white face with orange hair looming over me. Joujou was making love to me, not Chris. But I was too drunk to move or protest, and to escape I just closed my eyes.

—Thirst woke me up. It must have been near dawn, for the room was bathed in pale light, and I could see Chris's naked body beside me. I half-rose, still dizzy, with a splitting pain behind my eyes. I reached out to touch Chris's thigh, then my eye traveled up to the head buried in the pillow, and

I saw the white cheek and the corner of the red lip. He was still wearing his face makeup, and I was suddenly filled with great tenderness for him. I had what you might call a moment of insight. Joujou really *was* Chris. Joujou came from his interior life, and if I loved Chris, then of course I loved Joujou, too.

—Good for you, Laurie said. That's exactly right.

Vicki's hair had fallen partly across her eyes, shielding their expression.

—But my head felt funny, she said, and it wasn't just because of my hangover. I reached up and touched something strange, like a cap over my own hair, then brushed my forehead. My skin felt caked and stiff.

—I quickly got out of bed. I almost stumbled on my cat costume, which was crumpled on the floor, but I grabbed the edge of the dresser in time. The bathroom tile felt like ice under my bare feet. I groped around for the light switch.

—A clown face stared back at me from the big mirror over the double sinks. It was a big, hideous, white face with a huge, grinning, red mouth and blue-ringed eyes that were dripping painted tears. A bright pink spot glowed on each cheek. My long hair was tucked up into a curly orange wig. While I was passed out there on the bed, Chris had applied makeup to my face, and turned me into a clown.

—I looked at the rest of my naked body, perfectly human and attractive. I might have screamed if my mouth hadn't been so dry. I made a croaking noise in my throat.

—My God, Laurie said.

—I just stared at the clown. I thought I must be dreaming and pinched myself. But I wasn't.

—What did you do? Martha whispered.

—I picked up Chris's can of shaving lotion, and I sprayed it all over the mirror until I couldn't see the clown anymore. Then I flung the wig in the garbage and got in the shower. I scrubbed all the makeup off and washed it down the drain.

Then I went back into the bedroom for my cat costume, and I put it on, minus the tail and whiskers. Chris was still sleeping. I left the house, and later in the day I called him and told him I never wanted to see him again.

—Didn't you let him explain why he did it? Laurie asked.

Vicki smiled. Nope, she said. And that's the end of my story. Now I've really got to take a piss.

She yawned and stretched her arms above her head. Then she got up, and on her way to the ladies can, she passed close to the table where the man with the grizzled hair was sitting. They looked at each other and smiled. We knew that soon she'd be telling us all about him.